To Dakota,

M. K. Wood

piper's pond

*You are never too old to
believe in fairies...
You are never too old or
too young to believe
in yourself.*

◆ FriesenPress

Suite 300 - 990 Fort St
Victoria, BC, Canada, V8V 3K2
www.friesenpress.com

ISBN
978-1-4602-7837-6 (Hardcover)
978-1-4602-7838-3 (Paperback)
978-1-4602-7839-0 (eBook)

1. Juvenile Fiction, Fantasy & Magic

Distributed to the trade by The Ingram Book Company

A story written for my children Brody and Skyler, based on our made up bedtime stories. The journeys we went on, made my world that much brighter, and our laughter fills my heart.

You also taught me some valuable lessons along the way. Wherever your journeys may take you, remember that I have always believed in both of you. Follow your hearts, be kind, generous, respectful, truthful, and loving along the way. Always believe in yourself and don't let anyone try to change who you are. Brotherly and sisterly bond, when you stand together you are even stronger.

I love you beyond the stars and moon...forever.
Love Mom

xoxoxoxoxoxoxoxoxoxoxoxoxoxoxoxoxoxoxoxoxoxoxoxoxoxoxoxoxoxoxoxo xoxoxoxoxoxoxoxo

P.S. thank you for breathing life into this book!
Shout out... to all your friends and mine!

Chapter 1

Flopping onto her bed with her arms wide open, Skyler let out a huge sigh. Today was *literally* her last day in middle school. Come September, she would be going to high school, and the very thought of it made her cringe a little. It didn't help that she and her friends, once in a while, watched movies based on "cliques" in high school. In these movies, the girls thought of themselves as being super-hot; they were self-centred, superficial liars. *Seriously, what's the point? It always ended up badly for them. Or at least in the movies it did!*

Skyler had lost a few friends in middle school, because all they wanted to do was party, get wasted, paste makeup on, and dress like they bought their clothes from *Baby Gap*. She didn't have all the answers to growing-up, but what she did have was self-respect and respect towards all living creatures. It didn't matter what others thought about her. She liked herself for who she was.

At 13 years old, she enjoyed playing her guitar, reading, flipping through teen magazines (for the quizzes), and fashion. She was never drawn to the streamline trends. Skyler liked what she liked, even if it wasn't the so-called "in thing" at the time. Trends were in and out all the time, and recycled over the years. *Some styles should NOT be repeated! Like 80's fashion!* According to her mother, she had been self-assured and strong willed from a very early age. At two years old, she had begun picking out her own outfits. She thought back to one particular winter day, when her mom had taught her a valuable lesson about dressing appropriately for the weather. One early school morning, in Grade two, she walked outside in the middle of winter with just her fairy costume on. She loved that fairy costume! She still remembered the velvet bodysuit, covered in tiny pastel fairies, and the baby pink tutu. Skyler had complained to her mom about putting on her coat and boots. They totally didn't go with her costume! So her mom had let her go outside. Her feet had barely hit the snow, with the wind swirling around her, when she ran back into the house. Without a single word from either herself or her mom, Skyler slowly put on her coat and boots. Her mom was sneaky that way, saying things without saying anything at all! In the end, Skyler wore her fairy costume that day, and several days after. It remained a favourite until it no longer fit her—although, of course, she'd made some minor fashion adjustments, along the way.

Even with her haircuts, she was very specific about what she wanted. She thought back to when she used to print off the styles she really liked. When it actually came time to explain, however, or hand over the picture to the stylist, she couldn't do it! She would always turn shy, and look over at her mom for help. Until she was seven years old, she would always break into tears on their way home from the stylist. It wasn't that she hated the style; she was just sad for her hair, which had been left on the floor! She felt bad for the hair on the ground, being swept away and thrown into the bins! *Well, then again, at seven years old, I also believed my animals came alive at night, to protect me!*

At around that same age, she remembered seeing a movie, *Aquamarine,* with her mom. The mermaid in the movie had a cool aquamarine stripe through her blonde hair. *Who didn't want to be a mermaid or a fairy?* That's when she started to use non-permanent powder colours, which easily washed out of her natural blonde hair.

Lying on her bed, looking at her badly chipped nails, Skyler thought about searching *YouTube* for tutorials on makeup tips and nail art. She stared up at her ceiling, which was covered in posters of TV and movie actors and her favourite boy band, and tried to decide on what she wanted to do. Books had piled up on her bedside table and on the floor of her room. She had already read most of them, or was partway through, and for a brief moment, she thought about burying herself in one of the books.

She was feeling tired and her head started to spin with too many thoughts. *Ugggh ... hormones are a pain!* Flopping her head back onto the bed, with her legs hanging off the mattress, she watched Blue, her hamster. Her mom had given him to Skyler for her 10th birthday. She had done a ton of research on hamsters: proper care, proper food, proper cage, and proper grooming. Blue genuinely got excited when he saw her.

"Hey Blue," she smiled at him. He looked over at her with his little dark, dotted eyes peeking out at her from his fluffy beige and white fur. Then he turned away, but looked back at her one more time before fluffing up his fur, circling his bed twice, and then curling up to sleep. *Must be nice to fall asleep just like that*, she thought.

Glancing just above Blue and out her bedroom window, her eye caught a flickering movement from the corner of her room. Feeling too lazy to move the rest of her body, she lifted her head off the mattress, craning her neck to get a better view. She noticed a piece of shining purple foil, caught in the air vent on the floor and blowing around. Finally, she twisted her body and rolled onto her stomach to get a better look. She wondered if it had fallen off of something in her room. She looked up at the high shelf above it. All of her Webkinz (another craze in her life) were lined up on the shelf, and she smiled at the sight of them. They had very special meaning for her and her mom.

She fondly remembered her mom's stories.

As a dreamer, her mom always loved to make up stories, and most of the times, they included her collection of Webkinz. Skyler would pick one of them off the shelf—or sometimes a few of them to have more characters. At bedtime, the ones she picked would be the stars of the story that night!

At the very end of each story, her mom would swoop her hand around, circling the magical air over her face! By doing this, her mom grabbed all of Skyler's nightmares into her closed fists, and threw them out the window. Every night Skyler would convince her mom into staying longer by asking her to sing songs. They would cuddle under her blankets while her mom sung random songs (often getting the lyrics wrong) until she fell asleep. Skyler smiled at the memory.

"Whoops!" She sat up abruptly. She remembered that she needed to text her mom, to let her know that she was home safely. She slowly dragged herself off of her bed and walked over to her backpack on the floor. Unzipping it, she reached in to get her phone out, and quickly texted her mom:

Hola Mother, I am home safely. I love you ☺

Texting the word "love" made her wonder if her mom would ever find love again. It was just the two of them now. Her father had been killed in a drunk driving accident. Some stupid drunk teenagers swerved and hit her father at a pedestrian crosswalk. Her grandmother had told her once that he had died instantly on impact. The teens had been caught and arrested, but it didn't matter. It still left her without a father, and her mom without a husband. Skyler had only been one year old at the time.

She had pictures of her father, but no actual memories. Her family life with her mom was the only one she remembered. Her mom never remarried, and when she spoke about Skyler's dad, it was always with love, sincerity, and admiration. Deep inside, Skyler felt that her mom's heart had not quite mended. She always felt like her mom was waiting for something or someone. Skyler was working on a speech to give her mom about finding love again, but she knew it had to be perfect and the timing had to be right. Skyler's thoughts were interrupted by her text notification: a voice that sang out, *"It's your mom calling!"* She looked down at her phone and read:

Hola daughter! Thanks for letting me know. Just picked up a couple things from the grocery store. See you soon! Love you tons! Xoxooxoxoxoxooxoxoxooxoxooxooxoxooxooxoxoxoxoxoxoo xooxoxooxoxooxoxooxooxoxooxoxoxooxoxoxooxoxoxooxox ooxoxoxooxoxoxooxoxoxooxoxoxooxox

Her mom always went crazy on the x's and o's!

Skyler checked the rest of her texts from her friends, and replied back to some that actually needed a response ASAP. Some were about a fashion crisis, some were about boys, and some were about both. She scrolled down the news feed on *Facebook* and *Instagram*, and checked her *Snapchats*. She closed all her *apps* then and sat at the edge of her bed, absent-mindedly twirling her phone. In her peripheral vision, she noticed the purple foil again. Setting her phone down onto the bed, she went over to the corner of her room. Bending over, she slowly pulled it away from the vent, careful not to rip the foil. *It must belong to one of the Webkinz.* Skyler held it up to see it better in the light. The purple foil was no bigger than her palm, and she was surprised to see writing on it, in sparkling diamond ink:

One Entry Pass into Piper's Pond

June 28th
(One day offer)
Departure: 11:00 am
Leaving from: 244 Sunflower Rd.
(Jazz will be your bus driver)

Yours Truly,
Solarlite

"Okay, wait ... what?" Skyler breathed out loud, reading the ticket over and over again. "The 28th is tomorrow! Is this for real?" she asked out loud, as her heart began to race.

"Is what for real?" Skyler heard her mom's voice ask from behind her. She turned to see her mom leaning against her bedroom door. Skyler let out a startled scream! "Holy crap, Batman! Mom, you scared me! When did you get home?" She realized then that she was breathing really heavy.

"My bad!" This was one of her mom's favourite sayings. "I got home a couple minutes ago," she confessed. "I was in the drive-way when I texted you," she said, giving Skyler her warm, genuine smile, which always lit up a room. Skyler returned the exact same smile.

"So?" her mom asked, still smiling and nodding down at the ticket in Skyler's hand. She looked down at the ticket, then back up to her mom, and then down again at the ticket. After reading it again, Skyler handed it over to her mom. As soon as she read the first line, her mom started beaming like a wide-eyed child, and by the time she finished reading it, the smile had spread all the way across her face.

"Well, so what do you think?" her mom asked her, handing the purple ticket back to her.

"Seriously? I don't know what to think. You?"

"I say we talk to Jazz in the morning," her mom answered, matter-of-factly, and turned towards the door, leaving Skyler's room with a wiggling walk. She waved with an exaggerated hand-gesture, fanning her face and saying, in her best Southern Belle voice, "I do declare, it is time for me to make dinner."

Amazed at this response, Skyler went chasing after her, waving the ticket. "Hello! A little help over here, Mom?"

"My, my, it's going to be a beautiful day tomorrow," she said, still in full character, and still pretending to fan herself. "Yes, such a beautiful day, I do reckon." Her mom was wiggling her way to the kitchen, with Skyler hot on her heels.

"MOMMM!"

Chapter 2

Skyler woke up to the warmth of her mother's hand, gently stroking the side of her face. "Morning beautiful; it is 9:45am," she whispered into her ear. "Let's have some breakfast and get ready before Jazz arrives."

Then, all at once, the memory of the ticket came rushing back to her. She shook her head, as if to clarify her memory. *Right, we decided last night to meet the bus driver together tomorrow morning. Tomorrow? TODAY! Is this for real? I'll ask a zillion questions! Okay maybe not a zillion, but a LOT!* Skyler bolted upright, and her heart was pounding.

"Or you could get up that way, I guess," her mom said, startled by her instantaneous wake up/freak out. "You have lots of time; no need to freak out," she whispered, using her fingertips to brush one side of Skyler's sweaty hair away from her face. "Okay, so breakfast. I'll see you in the kitchen," her mom said, and turned to leave the room, "and remember to breathe."

Once she was alone, Skyler took a deep breath. "Okay," she said out loud, "you don't even know if this is for real." But curiosity, adventure, and excitement were brewing inside her. She kicked off her quilt and went into the kitchen. The radio was on and her mom was dancing around the kitchen, beating some eggs in a colourful ceramic bowl.

She greeted her, "Hello daughter! Breakfast is actually not good to go yet, probably another fifteen minutes. You can hang here, or get ready, it's up to you." Her mom continued to dance around on the kitchen floor's smooth colourful tiles. "Nice moves, Mom!" Skyler told her mom, over the music. Then she shook her head and laughed, "Okay, I'm going to get ready and have a shower."

"Okay great, because I'm pretty sure breakfast won't actually be ready for … 25 minutes!" There was silence for a moment, and then she heard her mom sing out, "My bad!"

Jumping into the shower, Skyler went over and over, in her head, what she was going to wear. *Maybe they give out t-shirts? What do I have to wear?* While towel-drying her hair, she decided on her comfy black tights, and a blue crop top with a white wolf on it. With one last look in the mirror, she whipped her wet hair up into a bun.

When she arrived back in the kitchen, breakfast was on the table in the little kitchen nook, which was moon-shaped with softly padded bench seating. The turquoise cushions had tiny stars and moons on them, and there were four throw pillows, each with a different coloured fairy. The nook had a full pane glass window that looked out over her mom's fairy garden. Her mom had created the garden quite a few years ago, with a little pond and everything, before Skyler could even remember. She added something new to it every year, so it had grown larger over time, and even more beautiful.

At night, Skyler would watch the solar fairies twinkle and glow. Her mom always had a thing for fairies, as far back as she could remember. She looked over at her mom, who sat joyfully looking out the window and enjoying her breakfast. *NO wonder Mom is excited about this ticket!* Eyeing the breakfast pizza, Skyler realized that she was starving! It was also one of her favourites. She looked down to see that her mom had already put a few slices on her plate. Her grandmother had given the recipe to her mom years ago, and for Skyler, it was a happy comfort food. On the table, there were also three floral-patterned china bowls filled with raspberries, bananas, and watermelons slices.

"Okay," her mom said to her, "we have about 30 minutes before the ETA time."

Skyler nodded over to her mother, but she was still looking out the window. She was starting to feel nervous and wondered if her stomach could manage food. The delicious smell from the breakfast pizza soon won over her hunger, so she picked up a slice and ate. *Yum!* Skyler and her mom sat in silence, eating their breakfast, and staring out the window at the fairy garden.

Her mom reached to open one of the side panel windows, which was decorated with a dragonfly, a shooting star, and a hummingbird drinking nectar from a flower. It was made out of colourful gels—one of Skyler's earlier crafts projects. Her mom pushed the window open. "Good morning!" Her mom sung out to the garden, waving to the fairies. For as long as she could remember, this was a ritual her mom did every morning and night. She had asked her mom once why she did this. Her mom had answered, "Because, they are happy to see us." Skyler knew that other people probably wouldn't understand why her mom talked to her "fake" fairies, or maybe they'd just think that she was a little bit crazy. Still, when she thought her mom might forget to greet them (not that she ever did), she would remind her. Skyler secretly felt protected by her mom's fairies in the garden. She thought about all the times they had spent in that garden over the years. Sometimes they would sit on a blanket, under the willow tree, and her mom would make up stories about the fairies there.

"Good morning!" she sang out, mimicking her mom's tone.

Her mom smiled over at her, and then her eyes widened! She was looking above Skyler at the moon clock on the wall. "Ten minutes!" she shouted excitedly, jumping up from where she sat and then running off to her bedroom. Before Skyler even started to really clear the table, her mom was back! She was wearing her overall jean shorts, and a red tank top with the word *candy* written in white. She had swooped her wavy blonde hair up into a messy ponytail, and strands of hair fell around her face. She was only five feet tall, and from a distance, looked like a kid! Skyler was already taller than her, but they had the exact same colour of blue eyes.

"Okay, do you have everything you need?" her mom asked her. "Your ticket?"

"*Hello!* We don't even know if this is for real," she replied. But she had the ticket anyway. She had tucked it into her tights, right after she got dressed.

"Let's just go with the assumption that it is," her mom suggested.

"Shoes!" she then said, excitedly. "Let's go wait out front." She looked like a teenager in that moment. *She often acts like one as well*, Skyler thought, while she followed her mom. She was almost skipping to the front door, and not bothering to put her own shoes on!

"Come on!" her mom said, looking so excited that she likely had to pee.

Skyler slipped on her blue canvas shoes before following her mom down their dirt driveway. On either side of their driveway ran two short stone walls, with wildflowers peeking through some of the cracks. Gargoyles, dragons, and angels were perfectly placed along the flat tops of the walls. Each one held a glass ball (the size of a tennis ball), and at nighttime they glowed, guiding her along the driveway.

Skyler was watching her mom skipping up ahead, and caught glimpses of her mom's fairy tattoo peeking out from her clothes. The tattoo, according to her mom, had just suddenly appeared one day!

Like, suddenly appeared? Come on! Skyler thought this while watching the fairy tattoo appear and disappear behind the straps of her mother's overalls.

It was a fairy with bluish hair blowing in the wind, casually sitting on an orange, quartered moon. Her wings were

13

breathtakingly beautiful and grand with turquoise hues. She had on purple pants with small swirls on it. There were shapes outlined in the larger part of the fairy wings: a wolf and a tiger. Two split-feathered tails continued farther down her mom's back from the lower wings, and ended in two feathered leafs, each with a zodiac sign: Leo and Pisces. These were the zodiac signs of Skyler and her father. She was still staring at her mom's back when her mom stopped suddenly, and Skyler almost ran into her. "Whoa!" she yelled.

Her mom grabbed her hand for the last few feet of the driveway. "This is so exciting!" her mom exclaimed, and squeezed her hand. Skyler didn't know if she was more excited or her mom, but right then it seemed like her mom was winning. They stood at the end of the driveway, holding hands. She took in a huge deep breath when she saw a bus coming down the road. It was apparently real. *No way!!!!* She yelled to get her mom's attention, "Mom! Remember, lots of questions; it could be a psycho!"

"Of course, I wouldn't just let you go *wherever*, or with *whomever*!" Her mom rolled her eyes at her. One time, the two of them had actually tried to stop the eye-rolling thing, but had failed miserably! Her mom started giggling

"You okay, Mom?" Skyler asked her, rolling her eyes in response.

The bus kicked up dirt along the country road, driving closer to where they stood, tightly holding hands. As it neared, the bus honked! Actually, it was more of a happy musical ditty, than a honk. The short bus, splattered with colourful paint, stopped right in front of them, and Skyler held her breath. *This is really happening.* The bus was covered in paintings: flowers, a sun, hummingbirds, dragonflies, shooting stars, waterfalls, moons, fairies, and people's names. The sound of the bus door opening made her jump. A plump dark-skinned woman, with long multi-coloured ribbons threaded through her dreadlocks, sat in the driver's seat. She was an older woman with a kind and gentle face, and wore a loose, rainbow tie-dyed dress.

"Good morning Piper and Skyler!" the driver cheerfully greeted them.

"Good morning Jazz!" Skyler's mom excitedly shouted over the bus's engine. Jazz turned the engine off. Skyler glanced from Jazz to her mom.

"Do you two know each other?" She was so confused. "And Mom ... your name is *Piper?*"

She knew her mom's first name. It was Madonna. The name was a tradition in their family. Skyler was the 5th generation of Madonnas. Her name was Madonna Skyler, but she was called by her middle name. Apparently her mom's middle name was Piper.

What gives? Crap, why can't I remember Mom's middle name? She rolled her eyes at herself. *Probably because I call her Mom!*

"Umm ...yes, we know each other, and Piper is my middle name. Hello? I've told you this a zillion times!" she answered, and then sheepishly smiled at Jazz.

"Your mom and I are old friends," Jazz softly told her; she spoke with a Jamaican accent.

"Mom?" Skyler questioned, hoping she would elaborate.

Her mom turned to her and hugged her tightly. "You, my beautiful daughter, are going to have one of the best days EVER!" Her mom was smiling so hard that Skyler thought her face was going to freeze that way.

She leaned in and whispered, "You are in good hands, and there is nothing to worry about. Just have fun and I will see you soon."

"I guess the zillion questions are out?" Skyler grunted from within her mom's tight hug. "You're not going to tell me anything else, are you?"

Her mom released her from the hug and gently kissed her cheek. Then she replied, dreamily, "We will have much to talk about when you get home. I love you. I'm *really, really sorry* that I couldn't give you any more information last night; I didn't want to ruin the surprise. By the way ... surprise!" She waved her hand towards the bus and Jazz.

With that, her mom hopped onto the bus and gave Jazz a big hug, "Take care of my girl, Jazz. So great to see you again. Say hello to everyone at the pond for me, please."

"You know I will, Piper. I have missed you!" Jazz said sincerely, hugging Skyler's mom tightly back. They hugged each other for a few moments more, before Piper turned and jumped off the second step of the bus. She squeezed Skyler again, and whispered how much she loved her.

"All ABOARD!" Jazz sang out.

Skyler hesitated a moment, looking back at her mom from the first step. She was beaming back at her.

"Can't you come with me, Mom?" she asked her.

"This is a journey just for you. We will have many more together, that I promise you." Her mom was still smiling, but this time with tears in her eyes.

"Mom?" Skyler asked, with concern in her voice.

"Oh these," she said, gesturing to the tears on her face, "happy tears, trust me. VERY happy tears."

"You know Mom, this all seems too crazy."

Her mom was beaming at her, and nodding in agreement. Through her tears, she mouthed, *I love you so much*, and held both of her hands over her heart. She heard Jazz sing out a Bob Marley song from behind her: *"Don't worry ... about a thing ... 'Cause every little thing ... gonna be all right."*

Skyler laughed. This was her mom's "go to song", whenever Skyler worried about anything.

"One more time!" Jazz chirped out and her mom joined in for the second round of the chorus: *"Don't worry ... about a thing, oh no! ... 'Cause every little thing ... gonna be all right!"*

Skyler got settled in her seat and Jazz started the bus up again, closing the door behind her. Skyler stared out the window at her mom, as the bus gradually pulled away. Her mom was still jumping up and down! She was waving at her with both hands over her head, and then bringing them down to blow kisses at her. She watched her mom until all she could see of her was a speck.

Jazz was a bundle of energy, asking her all kinds of questions about her friends, school, her interests in music, movies, TV shows, and just about everything else. Skyler had a hard time keeping up with Jazz's questions. She was mapping out the route of the bus and trying to make sense of why she was even here. She only trusted Jazz because her mom trusted her. It seemed so surreal. Just then, a huge gust of wind kicked up the dirt on the road, making a sandstorm! Looking out the window, the only thing she could see was a blanket of sand and nothing else.

"Hang on! Here we go!" Jazz exclaimed. A flash of blue light blinded them for a brief moment. Skyler, tried blinking her eyes a couple of times to adjust them. Suddenly, the blue light and sandstorm were gone, replaced by a huge forest! The bus kept humming along a narrow dirt road. The sun was shining through the trees; streams of sunbeams bounced the light around, making it look like someone had placed diamonds throughout the forest. The bus started slowing down when they approached a thick wall of trees.

"Almost there," Jazz said

"Where?" asked Skyler

"Piper's Pond, of course!" Jazz answered

Right. That's what the ticket said, duh… "You mean it's an actual place?" Skyler asked. *Wait a minute … Piper? Is it my mom's place? Or named after her? Or was she named after IT?* She would ask her mom these questions later when she got home. *IF* she got home!

"Of course!" Jazz exclaimed. The bus came to a stop in front of a huge wooden gate.

"Woo hoo! We are here!" Jazz said excitedly.

Large purple letters on the huge oak gate read:

Welcome to Piper's Pond

Beautiful vines were etched into the oak. Skyler stared at the enormous gate through the bus window. *Wow!* Jazz leaned over the back of her driver's seat and asked her if she still had the ticket. Tearing her eyes away from the gate, Skyler reached into the side of her tights and unfolded the purple ticket. "Fantastic!" Jazz cheered and continued with further instructions. "You see that large handle, the one that looks like a silver wolf?"

Skyler scanned the large gate until she saw what Jazz was talking about. Her eyes settled on the silver wolf, and she gave a slow nod without looking at Jazz.

"Great, take your ticket and feed it into the wolf's mouth … then presto!" Jazz exclaimed.

"Um, J-Jazz?" she stuttered, suddenly feeling nervous again.

Jazz seemed to sense her nervousness, and replied in song, changing the lyrics to a song from the movie *Dirty Dancing.* *"Yooou'll haave the time of your liiife..."*

Skyler shook her head. "Dude, seriously? What's with the show tunes?" She was half kidding and half not. But she was no longer nervous ... well ... not *as* nervous.

Jazz laughed hysterically at her question, and after catching her breath, said, "Wow! Pretty sure your mom asked me the exact same thing when it was her first time!"

"My mom? You mean she's been here before?" Skyler asked, her eyes widening with curiosity. Finally she asked the one question that was bugging her: "Is this my mom's place or is it named after her?"

Jazz avoided her question by busying herself with opening the bus door, pretending that she had forgotten how to do so. "Aha!" Jazz said, after a few moments, as though she'd made some grand discovery. With that, the bus door opened and she said, "Okay, time for your adventure."

"Way to avoid the question Jazz. You're not going to tell me anything more, are you?" Skyler asked her, tilting her head, and raising one eyebrow at her.

Jazz started to sing again. "*I can see clearly now; the rain is gone!*"

Clearly avoiding the subject! Skyler screamed inside her head.

"AHHHHHH … Okay, okay, I'm getting off!" she shouted over Jazz's singing.

"Have a super time Skyler; see you soon!" Jazz said, smiling at her.

Anything to get away from these singing telegrams! A person can only handle so many!

Jumping off from the second step of the bus, Skyler found herself facing the towering gate. Her jaw dropped. "*WOW!*" she gasped. After closing her mouth, she turned back towards Jazz, but she and the bus had already vanished.

"*Aaall byy myyyself!*" Skyler sang out, sarcastically, and jumped when she heard a howl cry out behind her! Mustering up all of her courage, she slowly turned back towards the massive gate.

Chapter 3

"Ahrrroooo!" The wolf's howl turned into a slight panting noise. The wolf's-head door handle was no longer solid silver; it was alive and panting like a puppy! It let out another howl, followed again by more panting. Its pink tongue was hanging out. The wolf was real, but there was just the head and shoulders! It seemed to be smiling at her. Skyler cautiously inched towards the wolf, squeezing the ticket in her sweaty palm.

"Hello," she whispered, once she was closer. The wolf was at her cheek level, so she could stare straight into its gentle and familiar sky-blue eyes. *Please don't bite me … please don't bite me!*

"Hi," Skyler greeted again, after clearing her voice of nervousness. With a much stronger voice, she asked, "Are you a girl or a boy?" *I'm standing in front of a real wolf, and asking it if it's a girl or a boy. Like it's every day that I come across a gate with a real wolf's head … nice Skyler … okay … and breathe.* The wolf's head had bobbed up and down in a nod when she'd said "boy".

"You're a boy?" she asked, for confirmation.

The wolf nodded again, and then *Slurrrp!* Puppy kisses. *Slurrrp!* This took Skyler by surprise and made her laugh out loud! She was giggling, "Okay, okay, good boy! You're so cute!"

She didn't feel nervous anymore and scratched behind his ears. The wolf kept licking her face. Skyler scrunched the wolf's face close together with hers, and said, lovingly, "Yes, who's the good boy? Yes you! Yes you are! You're so cute!"

"Ruff!" he replied.

They played back and forth for a while, giving each other lots of love. They were at home as wolf and girl. Skyler hated to admit that she even *had* a favourite animal, because she loved them all so much. Her love for animals ran deep, but when she was honest with herself, her favourite animal had always been the wolf. She and her mom called themselves animal whisperers! She thought about the week when her mom had camped outside with a grizzly bear. Her mom had told her that the bear was sick and needed her help. *Crazy!*

Her ticket had fallen onto the ground while she was playing with the wolf.

"Whoops!" she exclaimed, picking it up and examining the ticket for any damage.

"Ruff!" *Slurp!* The wolf continued to lick her face. He seemed to be trying to get her attention by widening his mouth, showing off his pure white fangs and pink tongue. Skyler knew what she needed to do, but it made her sad to think that she would have to leave him. She threw her arms around the wolf's neck and a couple of tears fell from her eyes. The wolf pushed into her, lovingly. She didn't want to leave him, but he let out a small whine, and opened wide again. "Okay, see you soon," she said, hugging him tightly. "I love you!" she said and really meant it. In return, the wolf gave her another wet side slurp! *Slurp!* Placing the ticket in his mouth, Skyler watched the wolf swallow it, instantly turning back into beautiful silver wolf, right before her eyes. She kissed the silver nose of the wolf, and moved away from the gate, which began to open.

Skyler waited patiently for the gate to open completely. Her eyes widened at the scenery behind it: a large emerald field with twinkling wildflowers! On the far side of the field stood a gigantic green hedge that disappeared into the clouds, and a stone path leading up towards *another* gate!

"Guess I'm not in Kansas anymore," she said to no one, knowing that it was a *cliché*. Skyler followed the sea-blue stones, and thought, *I wonder what makes those flowers twinkle?* A voice inside her head whispered to her, telling her to keep on the path. The gate was similar to the first one, but this time the handle was a silver lion's head the size of her fist! Etched into the wood on the right side was a maze, kind of like the hand-held puzzles she had done as a child—the ones with the rolling silver balls inside. Tracing her index finger along the puzzle, she weaved in and out of dead ends until she solved the maze. "Ta-da!" Skyler proudly said, making her index finger do a little bow at the success, "Thank you, thank you!"

"Well done, lassie!" she heard someone say. She jumped away from the door.

"No, no don't be afraid!" roared the Lion.

She looked over at the handle; the small lion was looking up at her, and smiling.

"Hello Skyler, my name is Desmond, a pleasure to meet you!" He spoke with a Scottish accent and looked like a real lion! But again, just the head and shoulders!

"Uh, hello Desmond … um ... a pleasure to meet you as well!" she greeted, but was still in shock that he was speaking to her!

"Aye, you will have a grand day!" he exclaimed. "Fantastic job on solving the puzzle!"

"You speak with an accent!" she said, pointing out the obvious.

"Aye, Scottish," he replied.

All she could say was "Oh!"

"Something a matter, love?" Desmond asked her.

"No, no, well I guess … it's just that I thought you would sound more like … um, kind of like Aslan from Narnia, or Mufasa from *The Lion King*." Skyler apologized then for making assumptions.

Clearing his voice with a small roar, he sang a tune from the Disney classic (actually sung by Timon and Pumbaa, not one of the lions): "I can see what's happening … What? And they don't have a clue … *Who?*"

"Oh no, not you too!" She groaned, slapping her head with the palm of her hand. "What is with the singing?"

Desmond cleared his throat again, with a larger roar this time. "Sorry, lassie. You don't like my singing?" he asked apologetically.

She felt bad for hurting the lion's feelings.

"You sing beautifully; you do! It's just today ... well there has been A LOT of show tunes going on today," she said, and reassured him that he was a lovely singer.

"Music is good for the soul, love," he said with a smile, looking at her with innocent lion eyes. Skyler couldn't resist the urge to reach down and stroke his head. Desmond began to purr like a kitten and pushed his head into her palm.

"I do like your singing," she said again, and scratched him under his chin. Desmond stretched his chin up happily, letting out a louder purr than the one before.

"Ah, ya hit the spot!" he purred. Skyler giggled at Desmond enjoying her affection. *PUUUUUUURRRRRRRRRRRRRRRRR!*

After a few moments, Desmond smiled dreamily up at her. "Thank you."

"Now what?" Skyler asked him, after she finished scratching under his chin.

"Whit's fur ye'll no go by ye!" he replied

"Huh?" she asked, not understanding anything he'd just said.

Desmond let out a deep laugh, as he translated, "It's an old Scottish saying, which means 'What's meant to happen will happen.'"

He continued, "You must redo the maze on the gate and push the sapphire button when you finish."

"But I didn't see a sapph…" Skyler trailed off when she looked back to the maze. Above the maze there was a quarter-size sapphire button with a picture of a fairy sitting on a quarter moon.

"When did that get there?" she asked Desmond, but there was nothing but silence. "Desmond?" She looked back to the lion, and saw that he had already turned back into silver. Just like she did with the wolf, she bent down and kissed the lion on the nose.

"Thank you Desmond, you really are a great singer," she whispered to him.

In less time than the first, she re-traced her way out of the maze with her index finger. "Okay, let's see what happens!" She held her breath as she pushed the button.

This gate opened a lot faster than the first one! Once she was inside the open gate, Skyler noticed even more green hedges. She hopped all the way in, quickly before the gate closed behind her. She had two ways to go: either left or right. *Oh no! I'm in a maze! Please don't be like Maze Runner … please, don't be like Maze Runner!* She told herself this over and over in her head. Flashes of the movie *The Maze Runner* went through her mind: Robotic-type monsters, trapped people, and a really messed up world (with *cute guys in it!*). She remembered telling her mom about the movie after seeing it with her friends. And when it came out on DVD, it was in her stocking the very next Christmas. She and her mom snuggled up on Christmas night with blankets and snacks, watching it in the dark. *The second one is coming out soon. YES!* Skyler thought, and did a quick fist pump. Then she realized, once again, that she really was stuck in a maze!

Oh, oh! The maze on the door flashed through her mind without any warning! Closing her eyes tightly, the vision appeared: the maze on the door, with her finger tracing through it. *Which way did I go first?* "Right!" she shouted. The smooth green hedges were perfectly straight and smooth, making it impossible for anyone to climb up them! At each branched-off pathway, she stopped, closed her eyes, and pictured the door in her mind. *Left, straight, left, right, straight, right, right, left, straight. Man the puzzle on the gate was much easier,* Skyler thought. She was pretty sure that she was nearing the end of the maze. Straight ahead, she spotted the gate! Running as fast as she could go, she was breathing heavy, and kind of enjoying the adrenaline rush!

Skyler reached the gate. This time the handle was a bear made out of gold, and about the same size as her fist. She searched the wooden gate for any hidden clues but couldn't find any.

"Hello bear," she whispered, secretly hoping the bear would come to life, like the lion had. *Zzzzzzzzzzzzzzzzz!*

The bear snored loudly. She gently stroked the side of the bear's face and softly said, "Helloooo?" The bear's smooth surface of gold turned to soft brown fur, and the bear blinked its eyes open.

"My, my, my, I do declare, I must have dozed off!" the bear yawned, speaking in a very feminine voice. Then she shook her head so hard back and forth that it made her fur poof out. "Why hello dear!" she said, suddenly realizing that she wasn't alone.

"Hello." Skyler smiled at the bear.

"My name is Audrey," the bear said

"Nice to meet you, Audrey. I'm Skyler. Did you have a nice sleep?" she asked her kindly.

"I dreamt that you were about to arrive," Audrey yawned again, baring her teeth, "and here you are!" She smiled warmly at her. She had a kind and loving, grandmother-grizzly look about her.

"My, my, yes, here you are; come over here and give me a kiss!" she said, making an awkward pucker. She spoke through her puckered bear lips, "Come on, give me some love."

Skyler tried to stifle her laughter, but couldn't hold it in. Still giggling, she bent over and gave Audrey the biggest kiss on the side of her cheek.

"Oooooooh child, *my* how you've *grown!*" Audrey exclaimed.

"Um … do I know you, Audrey?"

"No child, but I do know you," Audrey replied, with a smile and a wink.

"Now come, give Audrey one more kiss, because you," she paused for a moment before continuing, "you have quite the journey ahead of you. Promise to make the best of it and breathe child, breathe."

Skyler looked at Audrey and let her words sink in before bending down to kiss Audrey, one more time, on her cheek. Audrey didn't turned back into solid metal like the others had. "Will I see you again?" Skyler asked her.

"Dear child, of course, I am always with you. Always," Audrey said. "You carry me in your heart, as I do with you. Okay, you better get going; it's getting late and I'm going to cry." She sniffed, her eyes glistening, "And it is difficult to blow my nose. You just have to give the gate a little push open, that's all. Okay, one more kiss and you should be on your way; they are waiting for you."

Skyler gave Audrey extra kisses on her cheek before leaving.

A little ways along the dirt path, Skyler heard Audrey's growled words, loud enough to reach across the distance, "Ya'll have fun you hear! I love you." Turning back towards the gate, Skyler knew her voice would not carry with the power of a grizzly's roar, but she yelled anyways, with all her heart, "I love you too!" She hoped that her words reached Audrey.

They had.

Chapter 4

The grass was longer on both sides of her now, and the farther she walked the higher the grass seemed to get. "What the ...?" Skyler said. Spinning around to look up at the tips of the grass, she realized that *she* was half her normal size. Looking farther down the sunny path, she could see lights flashing in the distance, *greens, blues, purples, yellows, pinks, white* ... the colours went on and on! There were so many colours—more than she could name or had ever seen before.

Focusing on the lights, she walked towards them, feeling almost as though she were getting smaller and smaller the farther she walked. She shielded her eyes as she drew closer to them; the lights were unbelievably bright! She couldn't see any farther in front of her. Covering her eyes with both of her arms, she yelled a quote from *Gremlins*, an 80s movie that her mom had insisted she watch: "Bright light, bright light!" Certain movies quotes just stuck with her—even ones from her mom, and sometimes her mom misquoted A LOT.

Skyler heard a woman say, "Girls, dial down the lights; we're blinding her!"

"Dude, having trouble with that over here. Remember my wings are solar powered," said a young man's voice, "Oh and FYI … I'm *not* a girl!"

"Right, right, I know! Okay, on the count of three …" the woman's voice trailed off, being interrupted by a young girl's voice, which said, "Wait, wait! My light bulb has fallen loose; I need to tighten it."

"Dude," the same young man's voice said, "you don't even *need* the light bulb!"

"It keeps my legs warm while flying! Thank you very much!" the younger woman's voice huffed. "Oh, and I can turn my own light down when I want to; can you, Wave?" she bantered back. The blinding light was suddenly gone. A young man, and a young girl holding onto a large clear light bulb, landed directly in front of her.

"I'm so sorry about that; they are easily distracted," the older woman's voice told her. Skyler regained her eyesight from the bright lights and looked up. "My name is Sally," Sally said, hovering above the ground. Her wings were nearly invisible, and if not for the peacock feathers outlining the tips of them, Skyler wouldn't have even noticed them. Sally was wearing a forest green dress that flowed down past her ankles. Her thick, curly, dark hair flowed down all around her like a lion's mane as she landed. Skyler thought that she looked a lot like her grandmother's best friend. *Her name was Sally too! Hmm … coincidence?*

"Welcome Skyler, we are so happy you are here!" Sally said, and embraced her in a warm hug. The young man behind Sally was impatiently tapping his toes and whistling while he waited for his turn.

"Sky! Ssup?!" he asked cheerfully. "The names Wave! You come here often?" He laughed, giving her a hug and then winked at her. He was wearing baggy, tan surf shorts, and a baby blue muscle shirt with a print on it of a yellow wave.

"Check these babies out!" he said, taking a step back and spreading his large white wings out. They expanded, and on the inside of each wing played colourful images of surfers on the ocean. *Like a documentary on surfers!* Skyler watched in amazement.

"Like a 3D movie!" Wave told her.

"Okay, that's enough of that, show off!" said a young pretty fairy approaching Skyler. She was wearing a long black tube-top dress, with yellow splattered paint on it, and black knee-high socks. Her jet black hair was pinned up into two buns on the very top of her head. "Wave, hold this." She held her light bulb out to him.

Wave took it and brought it up over his head. "Look Beeze," he said to her. "I have an idea!" Wave laughed at his own joke. "Get it?" Wave asked, continuing, "A light bulb? Over my head ...? I have an idea!" He continued to laugh, while Beeze and Sally tried to ignore him. But Skyler could tell that they were trying hard not to giggle.

"You're such a child," Beeze told him. "You'll get use to him ... kind of," she told Skyler, while thumbing over her shoulder in the direction of Wave. Then she turned her full attention to Skyler. "So good to see you!" she grunted, hugging her. Skyler noticed, during their hug, that Beeze's wings were actually bee wings!

"My name is Beatrice," she told Skyler, "but my friends call me Beeze. So you can call me Beeze!"

"Dude, she doesn't say much does she?" Wave asked, nodding towards Skyler.

"Hush!" Sally scolded Wave. "It is a lot for her to take in; remember, it's her first time here," she said softly, "Isn't it dear?"

"Yes," Skyler nodded, unable to say anything more. It *was* a lot to take in. Then she finally asked them, "I'm sorry, but ... where am I?"

"Piper's Pond!" all three fairies sang at the same time.

"Well, just on the outskirts of the pond," Sally corrected.

"Oh! So I'm not dreaming or going crazy?" she asked.

"Wow! So much like your mother!" Sally exclaimed.

Wait till I get home! I'm going to ... okay, I don't know what I'm going to do yet, but I know that there will be a zillion questions this time! Mom can't hide!

"Duuuuuuude?" Wave interrupted Skyler's internal rant.

"Right, sorry ... just taking it all in. It's a bit overwhelming." *I AM going crazy!*

"Well it is about to get a wee bit more overwhelming ..." Wave's voice trailed off. A cluster of sparkles and soft lights were gathering around Skyler. She could feel the warmth from the lights on her skin, almost like a warm bath.

"Ooooooooh, this is so exciting!" Beeze squeaked out.

"What is?" Skyler asked her, with more than slight panic in her voice, not moving an inch. She was frozen in place. "What's happening?"

"Just wait. Don't worry; everything will be all right … seven, six, five," Beeze counted down, and the other two fairies joined in, "four, three, two, ONE!" A quick flash of fireworks exploded around Skyler.

"Ta-da!" Wave said, circling his arms wide and bringing them down as he bowed to her. "Aawwwesome!" He drew the word out.

"Wait, what do you mean ta-da?" she asked him, and looking at all of them for answers.

The three fairies only responded with *ooohs, ahhs, and wows,* and were staring at her with amazed looks on their faces.

The first one to say anything was Wave. "Totally, makes sense!" The other two just nodded in agreement.

"Um, hell-ooo? Over here? What makes sense?" Skyler was trying to get their attention for some answers.

"Wow!" Beeze breathed out.

"I agree, just beautiful!" Sally responded, with a continuously agreeable nod.

"Aroooooooooo!" Wave howled with his head tilted up to the sky.

Looking down at her outfit, to confirm or dismiss a growing fear, Skyler thought, *Nope, I'm not naked. Hey, where did my shoes go?* She looked around for her shoes and a white and silver wing slapped her in the face. "Ouch, what the—" She heard soft swooshing noises on either side of her, like eagles flying really low. Feeling

35

a slight breeze picking up, and hearing even stronger swooshing noises, Skyler dug deep, finding the courage to turn to her left. An enormous silver and white wing was attached to the back of her shoulder! She turned her head to the right and met the other enormous wing with her face. *Whappp!* (This was the sound of the wing and her face meeting each other.) "Seriously!?" Skyler shouted, rubbing the side of her face. The inside of her wing was lined with beautiful white wolf's fur. Even though it felt more like rabbit's fur, she knew it was white wolf, because between the slaps, Beeze had gasped out, "Look, the white wolf!"

Skyler reached out her hand to one of the wings, running her fingers along the inside of it, and the wing gently pushed back into her palm. *Whappp!* This time it was her other wing that struck her. "Really?" Skyler said, to the wing that gently swayed back and forth, looking innocent. The wing gently curled around her, and she noticed that her wings were layered on the outside with silver fur.

"It's okay! I know, I know! You just wanted some attention too," she said smiling, and ran her hand gently along the fur of the jealous wing. "There, there," she said, giving both of her wings equal attention. *Okay, I should be really freaked out by this ... how come I don't feel freaked out?* Looking to either shoulder, she couldn't doubt her own eyes. *Yep, I have wings. I should be freaked out.* Both of her wings wrapped around her.

Wave yelled, "GROUP HUG!"

Skyler was giggling, "Okay, okay, let's see what's going on here." She peeked out from beneath her wings, which were twice as big as her. They were dragging along the ground behind her, weight-less, feeling like her own arm or leg—a part of her. Sally, Wave, and Beeze shouted encores as she stepped out from behind her enormous wings!

"So what do you think?" she said, posing like a game show hostess, running her hands up and down both of her wings.

"Bravo, bravo!" Wave yelled, and acted genuinely excited.

"They're beautiful Skyler!" Beeze breathed. Beeze was so excited that she kept bending over, putting her hands over her mouth, and then back down onto her knees, smiling, "Wow!" she said, almost in disbelief. "I have never seen such gorgeous wings in all my days." She shook her head. "Wow."

Sally flew over to Skyler, with tears in her eyes, and hugged her.

"Okay, okay, I can't breathe!" Skyler gasped.

"I am so proud," she sniffed. "So proud." Sally walked back over to where Beeze stood.

"Thank you Sally," Skyler told her, "I just have to say, and I'm trying to figure out … should I be freaked out or not?"

"Dude, *you're* freaked out? Try seeing you from *my* angle; those are some gnarly wings, my friend," Wave said, while circling Skyler to fully inspect her wings. "Sweet ride."

Right away, he started to tell her about flying: What it was like to fly and what to watch out for. He even explained how wings worked in the wind. She couldn't wrap her head around all the advice and information. Up until now, she had still been trying to wrap her head around how she'd gotten here in the first place!

"Okay, start them up!" Wave instructed. "Try 'em out!"

"Excuse me?" She shook her head at him.

"Dude, your wings, try 'em out," he repeated, giving her two thumbs up.

"Oh yes, please do!" Beeze pleaded from behind him. Sally was nodding, but still sobbing near Beeze, overcome by emotion. Skyler held her breath, closed her eyes, and tried to remember some of what Wave had said. *Okay, so envision my wings moving ... move them like I move my arms and legs. Hmmm, I don't feel anything, maybe slightly cooler. I don't hear Sally crying, or Beeze ... or Wave!* Skyler opened her eyes. She looked down and screamed! A long, long way down in the far distance, she saw three fairies, barely identifiable!

"Okay, okay, okay, you're okay..." she kept repeating to calm herself. She was floating in the clouds. Gathering her thoughts and strength, she looked back at her wings. "I need you two," she said. "Work with me here! Now, I'm going to picture what I need you two to do. Okay?" The wings flapped twice, before tightly wrapping around her, protecting her body like an armour shield. She dove towards the ground until, a good 100 feet from the ground, her wings extended and she came to a nearly effortless stop.

Sweet! My own personal parachute! "Hey," she asked her wings, mischievously, "do you two want to try going up really fast?" In a split second, they reached the clouds and were floating in them. Skyler almost forgot that the other fairies were still waiting for her down below. Finally, she sang out, "*Going down!*"

Wave shouted to her on the way down, "SKYLER! Do a few loops! Pleeeeease, pretty please, a few nose spins and loop to loops!"

She tried out some of his requests, and then landed right beside Wave.

"Wow dude," he said, "your wings are so strong!" He petted the white wolf wing closest to him. "I've never seen anyone take to their wings so quickly. They mostly crash the first time!"

"Just beautiful!" Sally cried; she had finally stopped sobbing.

"Woo hoo! That was amazing!" Beeze exclaimed with excitement.

"Thanks, you guys," Skyler said, blushing from all the attention and excitement.

"Let's go show the King and Queen!" Beeze joyfully crooned. Skyler's heart sped up. *King and Queen!?*

She held her composure, as she questioned, "King and Queen?" Her voice squeaked a little as she said it.

"Of course! The King and Queen of Piper's Pond; don't worry, they are *soooo* nice," Beeze reassured her.

"Oh! I didn't realize there were kings and queens of ponds," Skyler said nervously.

"Nothing to worry yourself over, dear," Sally said, warmly. "Just one King and one Queen."

"They are AWESOME!" Wave said, with admiration in his voice.

He expanded his wings with a mission and looked over at Skyler. "I'll race ya!"

"There will be no racing to the pond today, Wave," Sally quickly told him.

"Aw," Wave sighed, pushing his bottom lip into a pout. "Fine, but we *are* going to race at some point." He gestured at her, pointing at his own eyes with two fingers, and then at hers. Then he repeated the gesture and made Skyler laugh.

"Oh yeah," he said, "we are on."

Clapping her hands rhythmically, Sally sang out, "Okie dokie, everyone ready?" With that, she extended her peacock wings.

"Almost!" Beeze said from the air. She was slipping her legs inside the clear light bulb, (with the missing cap) , and fastening it with a black and yellow stripe ribbon. Skyler could hear Beeze's wings buzzing behind her.

Before Wave took to the sky, he muttered over to Beeze, "Again with the light bulb?" Then he lifted off. "Are you guys coming or what?" he shouted down to them

"Coming dear," Beeze said sarcastically, flying to where Wave hovered.

"Are you all right sweetheart?" Sally asked Skyler, putting a gentle hand on her shoulder.

"I'm a bit nervous and confused," she told her honestly.

"That is understandable, but look how far you've already come," Sally said and gave her a wide genuine smile.

Skyler thought back to the wolf, the lion, and the bear. *Oh my! Guess I'm really not at home dreaming! Well, one good thing at least, there haven't been any show tunes in a while..."*

Wave couldn't have had better timing! He was flying in circles around Beeze, and started singing a Nelly Furtado song at the top of his lungs: *"I'm like a bird, I'll only fly away!"*

"Seriously?" Skyler screamed at him.

"What?" Wave asked, and continued to sing.

Chapter 5

Skyler flew through the air and tried some new tricks that Wave taught her along the way. "Watch this!" he shouted to her with excitement, and did four back flips in the air. "Whoa, a little dizzy," he held his head in his hands. Sally shot him a stern look. "What?" he asked, with an innocent look on his face. "It's not racing."

"Look Skyler!" Beeze said, pointing with excitement.

Scanning the forest up ahead, where the trees parted, she saw waterfalls pouring down from some cliffs that towered over the trees. *How could I have missed that?* They flew closer, and counted three waterfalls. One was snow white, the second was purple, and from the third waterfall crystal blue waters cascaded down. All three ran into a large pool with some type of movement happening around it. Floating too high above, she couldn't make out what was happening.

"Duuuuuuuuude..." Skyler heard Wave's voice as it trailed off; he had plummeted into a nosedive.

"Wait for me!" Beeze cried after Wave, who could no longer be seen. Beeze's wings let out a loud bzzzzzzzz, like an engine revving. "Coming!" she screamed and dove downwards after him.

"They really are ... easily distracted," Sally said, in a very loving motherly tone, "like most teenagers, but you can't help but love them." She sighed.

"Well, we better catch up to those two or they'll have everybody worked up about our arrival." She nodded down below, and took off after them.

Skyler hovered in the air for a bit longer, watching Sally become a speck in the distance. Needing a moment alone, she closed her eyes. Skyler could feel the wind and sun against her face. She could feel the sensation of her wings gently swaying back and forth. Taking in three deep breaths, exhaling, and then taking in three more, she thought, *Okay ... here we go.* Then she dove after the other fairies.

The three fairies weren't even halfway down before she caught up with them. They flew in a line together, right up until she gave Wave the same gesture he had given her earlier. Smiling over at him, she pointed to her eyes and then back at him; with that, she dove faster towards the ground. Wave took the bait and chased her down, but he ended up losing the race. She stood there waiting, with her hands on her hips, pretending to twirl her hair and whistle like she had been there for an eternity.

"*So* not fair! You had a head start!" Wave pouted, but then instantly brightened and yelled, "That was totally off the hook!"

"Skyler totally kicked your butt!" said Beeze, as she was landing.

When Sally landed, she half scolded them, "What did I say about racing?"

Wave tilted his head sideways, looking over at Skyler, pointing over at her with his thumb discreetly by his side. Skyler gave Wave an innocent look with wide eyes, as though it couldn't have been her who had really suggested it.

"I will let it slide this time, you two!" Sally said, looking from one to the other and trying hard not to laugh. Sally busily took out a *to-do list* from the inside of her green dress, while Skyler performed a victory dance for Wave. Beeze was laughing hysterically and Wave was back to challenging her again. Still in mid-swing of her victory dance, Skyler heard a woman's silky voice from behind her. "Hello Skyler." She knew who the woman was as soon as she turned around: *the Queen*. Breathtakingly beautiful, she wore a small crown made out of silver vines, twisted with real green vines and tiny ruby flowers. Long silvery hair fell below her waist. She wore a royal red dress that looked medieval, and yet somehow the Queen *made it look modern*. She stood much taller than Skyler. Her wings fanned out over a very large space on the ground behind her. *Swan feathers!* Her white silvery eyes sparkled into Skyler's. Then the Queen nodded.

Embarrassed that the Queen might have seen her victory dance, she thought she should say or do something, "Um, hello, sorry about that," she said, giving a miniature version of her dance followed by an awkward curtsy. The Queen laughed a warm and musical laugh. "It was a well-deserved victory dance," she said, smiling over at Wave, who blushed at her.

"Hello Sally, Beeze, and Wave," she said. "Fantastic job in bringing Skyler safely to the Pond." Sally and Beeze curtsied, while Wave awkwardly bowed. The three of them started laughing as they flew over to tackle the Queen.

"Group HUG!" Wave yelled, grabbing Skyler and pulling her into their hug. The Queen's soft wings wrapped around all of them.

"Welcome to Piper's Pond," said the Queen, looking down into Skyler's eyes.

"Thank you," she whispered back up to the Queen. *I like her!*

"The King will be so happy to see you!" she said, unwrapping her huge wings, and ending the group hug. Soon after the mention of the King, they heard whooping, laughter, and hollering. "Hello, hello! Welcome Skyler, welcome!"

The Queen laughed, "Speaking of the King," she said, looking into the sky, waving and smiling, "Hello dear!"

Fear hit Skyler when she spotted the King riding a killer whale across the sky towards them. It wasn't that she hated whales, she'd just had a huge fear of them ever since she was little. She had almost fallen into an aquarium, trying to see what was kept in one of the larger pools. Her mom had caught the back of her shirt before she'd fallen in, but not before a whale came literally eye to eye with her. Kind of scarred her for life (or so she thought). The fact that this whale was clearly magical, flying towards her instead of swimming, made little difference. She backed up, pushing her wings into the Queen's chest, retreating from the whale and pushing the Queen back with her. She felt the Queen's hands coming to rest gently on her shoulders. "It is all right Skyler. B.W. is really sweet."

She didn't know if the Queen was talking about the King or the whale. Still pushing against the Queen, she watched the King and whale slide to a stop. The whale hovered close to the ground, its fins acting as wings; Skyler's heartbeat was pounding so hard she could hear it. The King leapt through the air before her eyes, landing directly in front of her with a broad smile on his face. He leaned over her to give his Queen a gentle kiss on her cheek and another on her lips. "Hello, my lovely." The King wore shorts that looked like a home-made project, with a hem designed with zig-zags (like *Peter Pan's*). He had muddy bare feet, and his bare chest was covered in mud as well. Colourful fall leaves stuck to him and he was wearing a crown made out of twigs and branches! His black wings stretched out the length of a pickup truck!

"Dear, you are kind of freaking her out," said the Queen to the King, with her hands still resting on Skyler's shoulders. The Queen could feel Skyler's racing heartbeat through her fingers. "Whatever are you wearing?" she asked her husband.

He beamed at her. "The kids needed someone to play a tree." The King stepped closer and lifted Skyler's chin up with one of his mud-covered hands, so that he could look into her eyes. "Oh dear, you *do* have fear in your eyes. I am so sorry, I didn't mean to scare you!" he said sincerely. He looked at her with his soft grey eyes and folded his wings into his shoulders. Skyler took another glance over to see if the whale was still there. It was, and it was looking straight at her. She glanced back quickly into the eyes of the King.

"Ohhhh," he said. It was like he had read her mind, "B.W.?" he asked. She just nodded.

The whale's happy expression turned to a sad one, and she let out a sad cry. The King leaned down to Skyler *(He's massive!)*, and whispered to her, "Would you like to try and meet her? She was super excited to meet you today." She peered again at the whale, and then back over at the three fairies; Wave was encouraging her by nodding like a bobble head.

She had really liked the King right away and didn't want to offend anyone at the Pond. "I'll try," she squeaked out.

"At a girl!" He slowly and gently guided her over to B.W., who got so excited that she squirted water out of her air hole, soaking Sally, Beeze, and Wave, cracking everyone up—well almost everyone. Beeze let out a scream, "My outfit!" She stomped her foot and flew off to get changed, with her light bulb in her hand.

"Look Sky, it's no big deal," Wave said; he flew over to the whale. "Who's a good whale?" he asked, scratching under her fin. "*You* are! Yes, you *are*." B.W. squirted more water out. "B.W., hold your water steady for me!" Wave jumped up to where B.W. continued to squirt water for him, and tried surfing the water with his bare feet, until he lost his balance and wiped out. "Wipeout!" Wave yelled the obvious from the ground.

Skyler was still a good three feet away. B.W. glided over to her, stopping right before her, and Skyler held out her hand. She had her eyes closed the whole time; B.W. softly pushed her nose into her palm. The whale felt smooth like satin, but wet. Skyler opened one eye, and B.W. mimicked her, closing one eye. Skyler switched, closing her other eye and keeping the other one open in a wink. B.W followed suit.

Skyler opened both eyes and reached out to B.W. with both hands. Running her hands along the killer whale's torso until she reached one of her fins, she scratched B.W. under her fin, like Wave had done. *Whoooooooshhhh!* She and the King were soaked.

The King asked Skyler to ride together with him on B.W., and she accepted. One way to get over her fear was to face it. As they headed towards Piper's Pond, the King told her to call him Uncle Tomas or Tom for short. He also told her that B.W. was a girl, and said that her initials stood for Beautiful Whale. B.W. snickered at that, and so he admitted to Skyler that it actually stood for Blossom Water. The King continued to tell her that he had known the whale since she was a baby, born in the pond. "Isn't that right girl?" he asked B.W., as they glided in and out of the clouds.

Skyler felt the need to stretch out her wings as she hung onto the King, but before she could, the inside of her enormous wings caught the wind … forcing her backwards and making her lose her grip. She flew through the air a few feet behind B.W. and the King, and quickly regained control over her wings. She yelled over to them, "MY BAD!"

After making sure that everyone was okay, the King asked her if she wouldn't mind showing him some of the tricks she knew. The sensation of flying was quickly becoming a type of freedom for her. She happily obliged! The King and B.W. cheered her on with each trick, Blossom soaking the King a couple of times.

The King took a turn showing her a few more tricks—what he called, *REALLY cool ones!* His black crow wings shot out sparks and streams of colours. He made designs and paintings in the sky: mountains with rivers, sunsets, sunrises, mazes, animals, people, and exploding fireworks. Skyler's view of crows changed—almost. *Although actual crows are still rather annoying at times.*

The King hovered with his fully extended wings being lit from behind by the sun. He reminded her of the Greek God, Zeus, even wearing his tree costume and twig crown, with a few leaves still stuck to him (although some mud had been washed off by B.W.); he was a large muscular man with long snow-white hair, the same colour as his moustache and the beard falling below his waist. *A toss-up between Zeus and Ariel's dad in The Little Mermaid,* she thought to herself. Skyler petted B.W., while they watched and cheered on the show Uncle Tomas was putting on. B.W. tried carefully not to soak her, but failed a couple times during the fireworks.

When Uncle Tomas and Skyler finally arrived at Piper's Pond, and landed amongst the small gathering waiting for them, Wave asked, "Hey what took you guys so long?"

Skyler flew off B.W.'s back and landed in front of the whale's black and white face. She gently kissed her. "Thanks for the ride Blossom; it was fun," she whispered. Blossom gently pushed against her head and licked her entire face with a large pink tongue.

Skyler wiped her face with the back of her hand as she watched Blossom fly over to the pond and dive into its colourful surface to the waters below. A rainbow of colours shot up from where B.W.

had entered the water, followed by several scattering sprays that made a full-sized rainbow across the pond, fading into mist.

"So dear," the Queen spoke to her husband, "What *did* take you so long? Hmmm …?" she asked, but her tone gave away the fact that she already knew the answer.

"Bad weather, right Skyler?" Uncle Tomas looked over at her, and winked knowingly.

"Yeahhhh … bad weather," she echoed, but did not make eye contact with the Queen. Skyler had a hard time lying, in fact. Plain and simple, she couldn't lie; it wasn't in her nature. She broke when she finally made eye contact with the Queen, blurting out, "It was just so amazing!"

"Aw Uncle Tom, you did the show without me?" Wave complained.

"Next time Wave, I promise," Uncle Tomas said, patting him on the shoulder.

Tiny fairies appeared from behind a nearby willow tree and yelled excitedly, "Uncle Tom! Uncle Tom!" There were at least a dozen small fairies running and flying over to him. They all tightly hugged the King.

"Aw, you ruined the tree costume we made you," said a little girl fairy wearing a purple tutu and a white leotard. Her brunette hair was tied perfectly into a bun on the top of her head, and she was looking up at the King with bright green eyes. She fluttered her purple butterfly wings while she inspected the rest of his costume.

"You can make me another one, Tulia," he suggested to her.

"Hmmm," Tulia said, thinking over the King's suggestion. She looked deep in thought for a moment, and then squealed happily, "Maybe one with birds and nests!" With that, she spun and flew off in a hurry to make another creation. The rest of the children fairies hugged the King before they too flew off in the same direction as the purple tutu fairy, behind the enormous tree. Along the bark of the enormous willow, Skyler spotted several tiny wooden doors, and at the bottom of the tree, one large door.

She looked back towards the pond and the cliffs; the three waterfalls she had seen earlier now seemed even more enormous. *My eyes weren't playing tricks!* One was definitely crystal blue, one was white, and the other was pink.

Wait a minute! she thought. *The other waterfall was purple before!* She was sure of it. Closing her eyes, Skyler pictured the scenery in her head from before. *Yes, it was definitely purple.*

"You want to take a closer look?" asked Uncle Tomas with a nudge to her shoulder. Still staring at the waterfalls, she slowly responded with a slow nod of her head.

"Hi y'all!" Beeze cried out, flying towards them, this time without her light bulb.

Wave teased her, "Where's your precious light bulb?"

"I don't need it right now, Mr. Know It All," Beeze scoffed, and crashed into Wave so that he ended up on his rear end.

"Dude, OUCH!" he said, getting up and rubbing his backside.

"Okay you two, knock it off!" Sally huffed and continued to speak with the Queen. "I'm going to go get tea time set up and ready."

The Queen thanked Sally and said that she would be along momentarily to help her. Sally gave Skyler a hug before flying off.

The Queen glided over to her husband, kissed him on the cheek, and told him, "*Try* to behave dear." She turned towards Skyler, "Have fun Skyler, I know you will with these three, and I will see you at tea time." The Queen wrapped her wings around Skyler. Then she let her go and took flight, her swan wings creating a strong wind as she flew away. Skyler stared after the Queen with an amazed look on her face. *She soars with as much grace as a swan.*

"Race ya!" Uncle Tomas yelled, challenging everyone. Wave was looking around to make sure the Queen and Sally were out of sight. Then he became super excited, yelling from a crouched position, "Countdown! 10, 9, 8, 7, 6 …" Skyler and Beeze smiled over at each other during the countdown and then crouched down with him. Joining in, they all yelled. "5, 4, 3, 2, 1 … blast off!"

It was too close to call between Uncle Tomas and Skyler for first place. Wave and Beeze didn't even make it to the finish line. During the race, they cut each other off and crashed into a very large sunflower. "Re-do, Re-do, illegal move by Beeze!" Wave was shouting from where he lay on his back on the ground.

"Hey, you started it!" replied Beeze, after she stood up and brushed off the pollen from her dress and black knee-highs.

"No re-dos! You know the rules!" Uncle Tomas chuckled. He looked down at Skyler, "Simply amazing, I haven't had a close race like that … well, since my last race with my wife!" he exclaimed. "Extraordinary, I must say, especially since you are a new fairy; your wings are already so strong and you've become one with them."

Skyler looked up at him with her blue eyes and noticed for the first time that the King's eyes shone like the wolf's did at the main gate.

"I've only met one other fairy like you, and her name was—" he was cut off by Wave, who crashed right into him.

"Sorry Uncle Tom!" Beeze apologized with a curtsy and a sheepish look on her face. Beeze had charged Wave in mid-flight but accidentally made him fly awkwardly into the King.

"See what I mean Uncle Tom? I-l-l-e-g-a-l move!" Wave shouted over his shoulder to Beeze.

"Who? Moi?" Beeze asked innocently.

"Okay you two, enough of the horseplay," said Uncle Tomas.

"Sorry Uncle Tomas!" Beeze and Wave sang in unison.

Skyler heard someone whispering behind her "It's *her!* Skyler! You know, the one they said was coming today?"

"Wow, check out her wings!" said a louder girl's voice. "They're the white wolf! Pretty!"

"*Shhhhhh!*" whispered the first voice.

Skyler turned and faced the two young girls, who were in the pond, peering up at her from the water. "Hiya!" greeted the girl with fire-red hair.

"Your princess," greeted the other girl, who had raven hair. She flew out of the water and curtsied to Skyler. *Mermaids! What? Wait! Flying mermaids? No way! Wait ... What? Princess?*

"Hi," she answered back. "You're mermaids!" she exclaimed, knowing that she was stating the obvious, but unable to help herself. She loved mermaids as much as fairies and animals. And these were both fairy *and* mermaid! The red-hair fairy emerged from the waters, flying beside the other mermaid.

"Yes! Fairy mermaids," the redhead replied excitedly, and flipped her pale green tail with golden-flecked scales towards Skyler. The raven-haired fairy's tail was purple with flecks of baby blues.

"You are both very beautiful!" Skyler told them. The two fairies giggled and blushed at her compliment.

"G-I-R-L-S!!!!!" shouted an older woman's voice from behind one of the waterfalls.

"Oh, oh, Mom!" both mermaids said in unison. "We've got to go; we're preparing for the light show tonight. Bye Skyler!" They quickly disappeared into the pond.

"Wow, mermaid fairies!" she breathed.

"Dude … there's tons of different fairies at Piper's Pond," Wave told her. "You've got the whale fairies like B.W., mermaid fairies like the ones you just met, animal fairies, guard fairies, insect fairies, dragon fairies, tree fairies, garden fairies…" He kept listing off a ton of fairy types, until he finally ended with, "The best ones are water fairies LIKE ME!"

"Don't forget Bee fairies," Beeze added, and gave Wave a mean look, because he had forgotten to list her.

"I included you," he objected, "I said insect fairies!" He grinned.

Beeze gave Wave a solid punch in the arm. "Fine," he said, rolling his eyes. "Bee fairies."

"You will have plenty of time to meet all the fairies," Uncle Tomas assured her.

"Can we please do the pipeline today, Uncle Tomas?" Wave begged.

"Pipeline?" Skyler asked them.

"It is a rush, Sky!" Wave exclaimed, pointing over to the pink waterfall.

"Why are the two waterfalls white and pink?" Sky asked the King.

Beeze answered before the King could, "The white one is milk, great for the skin and bones," Beeze said, while examining her skin. "That other one changes flavour every few hours, and right now, my guess is that it's pink lemonade."

Wave ignored Beeze's explanation and kept pleading with the King, "Can we, can we, can we, please?"

"Why don't we ask our guest what she would like to do?" he asked Wave.

"Dude, are ya in or are you out?" he asked Skyler, "In or out?" he asked again, pumping his hands up and down as though he were lifting weights. "In or out?" His hands kept moving.

She couldn't help but giggle at how excited Wave was, so she nodded in agreement.

"Sweet!" he joyfully let out, flying over to Skyler in a sideways spin.

"Okay, do you like water slides?" he asked her with excitement in his eyes.

I love them! Skyler nodded to Wave.

"Most excellent! Let's go!" he shouted, grabbing her hand and pulling her up into flight. Wave guided her all the way up to one of the highest cliffs' edge, with Uncle Tomas and Beeze right behind them.

When they landed on the cliff's ledge, she noticed the massive forests surrounding Piper's Pond. It went on and on for as far as she could see. Lost in the scenery, she didn't hear Wave giving her instructions until he came right up close to her ear, and spoke with his hands cupped around his mouth. "Earth to S-k-y-l-e-r, come in Skyler! Are you there?"

"What?" she asked, a bit startled.

"I *said*, it's just like a water-slide but way cooler. Same thing, just give yourself a heave ho down and zooooooom!" He exaggerated the motion with his hands.

Skyler looked around and noticed what he was talking about: an entranceway to "The Pipeline". It did look like a water-slide, but it was made with river rocks and the water was pink.

"Best thing? If you swallow a mouthful during the ride, it will taste like pink lemonade," Wave said, right before launching himself down the tube, screaming, "Woooooooooooo hooooooooooo!!"

Eeeeww, she thought. *I can't drink it! What if someone peed in it?*

"It has a really good filtering system," Beeze said, matter-of-factly, "the water for the ride. Just in case you were wondering, and you swallowed some ... or if you're worried that Wave might pee in it."

"Okay ... good to know!" Skyler leaned over to see if she could see Wave splash into the pond but the view down below was blocked by rocky overhangs and different types of tubes.

Beeze yelled, "My turn!" She hesitated a moment, and then turned back, "Unless either of you two would like to go first?" she asked politely.

The King and Skyler answered, "No thank you, you can go."

Without any more persuading, Beeze was quickly well on her way down the slide.

Uncle Tomas chuckled and said, "I think you should go next." He read her mind then, and reassured her, "Your wings will be fine; they will adapt with you and they dry right away." Skyler realized that she had been staring back at her wings, and her forehead was scrunched up with concern.

Skyler winked at Uncle Tomas, before launching herself down the slide. The tube-slide started off a little dark, illuminated by a soft glow of twinkle lights. She slid slowly through another tunnel that glowed like a sunset over the ocean. The next tunnel shot her fast and straight into space, surrounded by galaxies, shooting stars, milky ways, a large full moon, and planets. The following tube was a large dome tunnel with bright blues, reds, yellows, and orange hues. *No wonder Wave loves this ride!* Looking around at the bright walls of the tube, she saw that the same surf video was playing on all the walls: surfers riding massive waves. Skyler came to a stop mid-tube; she stood up in ankle deep water right before a small gate, and saw that, to her right, there were a variety of surf-boards to choose from. She picked a small surfboard, similar to the one she had learnt to surf on when she was little. *Okay, here we go!* Large waves were coming towards her now, strong but manageable. Pushing the green button to open the gate below her, she walked down a couple of steps with her surfboard and paddled out towards the waves.

The surf tube lasted for quite a while. She rode one wave extremely well, letting out a really loud, "Woo hooo!" that echoed down the tunnel. Nearing the end of the last waves, a huge warning sign glowed brightly on the surface of the tube. In one picture, a fairy was sitting down, and in another, a fairy stood. The standing fairy was circled in red, and crossed out: **WARNING!** Skyler sat down before the tube narrowed again. She placed her surfboard into another lane beside her, when she saw another sign that read: *Surfboards In This Lane.* She spotted another warning sign above her, in bold letters, that read **"PLEASE LIE DOWN COMPLETELY"** and showed a picture of a fairy lying straight down on her back. She did exactly that and laid completely down. Nothing happened at first, but then she could feel herself speeding up and suddenly being launched through a loop to loop in a clear plastic tube. She caught glimpses of the sky and clouds whenever she slid halfway up the slide's walls. Then she drifted into another tube that led through calm waters. She was surrounded by a starry night in a meadow, with the sounds of frogs and crickets inside the tube. Then she slid through a field of wildflowers at sunrise, a rain forest, a safari, and different countries from around the world.

All of a sudden, she shot through a rainbow tube, and was spat out into a large body of water! This took her by surprise, making her swallow some of the water. *It DOES taste like pink lemonade!* she thought, as she half choked on it.

Beyond the roar of the waterfall, she heard Wave and Beeze whooping and hollering: "Woo hoo! Way to go Skyler! Come over this way!" She swam towards their voices, amazed by how light her wings felt in the water; she had expected them to weigh her down.

She easily reached the shore and Wave looked down at her. "You know, you could have just flown over here."

Skyler made a funny face at him as she climbed out of the pond.

Beeze quickly turned her to face the exit of the slide, and with a big *SPLASH,* the King did a cannon ball into the water!

"Uncle Tomas does something different every time! My absolute favourites are his belly flops," snickered Beeze.

"Woo hoo, Uncle Tomas!" Wave yelled.

The King's large hand waved over to them before he flew out of the water and over to where they stood.

"Skyler didn't know she could just fly out of the water Uncle Tomas," Wave said, with a childish undertone.

"I love swimming Wave, hell-oooo!" she said, mimicking his tone.

"Love that ride!" Beeze squealed.

"Me too," Skyler agreed. Staring at the slide, she couldn't quite follow the entire Pipeline the whole way up. It weaved in and out through the trees, and cliffs' edges.

"About an hour ride?" the King asked them.

Wave looked at his make-believe watched and replied, "Yep! About that."

"No, you're kidding, right?" Skyler asked with wide eyes. It seemed to go by so quickly!

Beeze answering her, "It usually takes about an hour or an hour and a half, or somewhere around there. I'm starving!"

Skyler had lost track of time, and honestly, time had not even entered her mind at all. Her stomach growled, interrupting her thoughts.

"See, Skyler's hungry too!" Beeze pointed out.

"TEA TIME!" the King announced to them. He clapped his hands, rubbing them together with anticipation.

"Dibs on the blue snow-cones!" Wave yelled over his shoulder, as he flew off in the direction of the willow tree.

"Oh, don't listen to him, there is plenty to go around," Beeze rolled her eyes after him. She reached out and grabbed Skyler's hand, "Let's beat him there!" Beeze suggested to her excitedly. She was squeezing Skyler's hand, with a huge smile on her face.

They both looked over to the King, who nodded at them, and said, "Go catch up!"

In no time, they had caught up to Wave. Skyler was pulling Beeze through the air with her, to speed her up.

"Noooooo wayyyy!" Wave said, with an astonished look on his face, which changed right away into a look of determination. He sped up a bit; it didn't take any effort for her to keep pace with him! Skyler could have easily passed him, but she didn't know where they were going.

"Skyler," she heard Beeze say, "straight down." Beeze was pointing down to a fairground with roller coasters and merry-go-rounds, and they could hear the sounds of music. The smells of cotton candy, popcorn, and hot dogs floated up to them.

"Land where the big target is; do you see it?" Beeze asked her. It was hard to miss! It was a large painted target on the ground with a huge red dot for the bull's-eye.

"If you hit the bull's-eye, you get a random prize," she said, smiling, and thumbed out her leather necklace around her neck, for Skyler to see. It had a black opal bee dangling from it! The colours from the opal stone made perfect yellow stripes, and the wings set in the opal were woven out of delicate gold. Two tiny gold gems sparkling for each of the bee's eyes.

"It's beautiful Beeze!" Skyler smiled at her, before they flew off past Wave again. He looked at them with wide eyes and mouthed the words *"No way!"* Skyler and Beeze hit the bull's-eye dead on. Wave almost missed the bull's-eye, but Beeze grabbed his foot in time, and pulled him down to the ground with them, making all three fairies fall to the ground in hysterical laughter.

They were laughing so hard that they hardly noticed the three dragons that had entered the bull's-eye. Skyler stopped laughing when she saw them. The three dragons reminded her of her Webkinz collection right away.

But these are real dragons

One was baby blue, shaped more like a sea horse than a dragon, but with a dragon's feet and wings. The second dragon was larger than the others, almost completely purple except for the stomach, wings, and horns! They were the colour of the pearls one would find in an oyster! The final dragon was pure white, though the skin sparkled with shades of soft blues, and her wings and stomach glimmered shades of silver. She had extremely long black eyelashes. *Definitely the Queen of the dragons!* Skyler thought.

Skyler noticed that each of the dragons held a small gift. The white dragon walked directly towards her. Holding out the small gift to Skyler, the dragon smiled and batted her long eyelashes at her. She carefully took the gift from the dragon, who immediately soared beautifully away through the skies and towards the carnival. She looked over at Beeze and Wave; both of them held a present in their hands. The other dragons had already taken off to follow the white dragon. *No way! I just met dragons!*

She could hear Wave rattling his gift; she looked over to see Wave and Beeze shaking their gifts while holding them up to their ears.

On the count of three, and in unison, Wave and Beeze carefully unwrapped their gifts. But right before the wrapping hit the ground, it turned into dozens of butterflies! There were no traces of wrapping paper remaining, just fluttering butterflies. Skyler's attention was quickly drawn away from the butterflies. Wave was super excited, holding out a gold pocket watch, and Beeze was busy looking at her own gift with deep affection. Beeze held out dangly earrings, which looked like bees and matched her necklace!

"Open yours, open yours!" Beeze cried out to Skyler, while she put her earrings in.

"I'll time you!" Wave said, looking down at his watch, "Go!"

Skyler carefully and gently unwrapped the small box. She lifted a silver charm bracelet from it and watched the gift wrap turn into butterflies again. She held out the bracelet in the palm of her hand. Seven charms hung from it: a miniature bus like Jazz's, a small carved opal maze with a teeny tiny rolling silver ball in it, solid silver musical notes, a silver wolf howling with a full moon behind him, a smiling silver lion's head, a gold bear with fur like honey, and a tiny pair of wings identical to her own: fur and all! Tears brimmed in her eyes. She looked over at the other two fairies, who were wearing wide smiles upon their faces.

"I love it," she whispered over to them.

Wave and Beeze came over and tightly hugged her. They took turns showing each other their precious gifts.

"Dude?" Wave questioned loudly to the sky, and back at Skyler's bracelet, "Seriously? What, no surfboard or waves or—"

"What? No bees?" Beeze interrupted. "That's okay, we will figure something out," she said, patting Skyler on the shoulder. "It's perfect for you!" She fastened the bracelet on Skyler's wrist.

"Race you guys!" Wave shouted, looking at his watch briefly and then flying off.

"Cheater!" Beeze cried after him, and giggled.

"Give me your hand again; we've got this," Skyler said confidently. She grabbed Beeze's hand. Shaking her wrist lightly, to feel the charms, she took off chasing after Wave. *This is the best prize I have ever won!*

Chapter 6

"So how come they call it tea time?" Skyler asked Beeze, after swallowing a bite of her hot dog.

"Well, see that tent over there behind the games? The tent with the huge flowers on it? It's a Tea House," she told her.

"It has fantastic tea, fingers sandwiches, and pastries!"

"We can go there later when we get hungry or thirsty again! But let's play some games and maybe go on some rides!" Wave said, rubbing his stomach. He had inhaled four hot dogs and two orders of chili fries, plus three snow cones!

They walked through the food stands and over to where the games were. Skyler noticed that they were similar to the games she had played at other fairs: basket throws with baseballs, water races with squirt guns (but instead of guns, the water here came from sea horses), ring toss, balloon darts, and the duck pond. But there were some she had never even seen before. Beeze and Wave had a favourite game they were looking for. Skyler could sense they were on mission, and she quickly had to catch up to them.

"Wings!" Wave said out loud, staring up at two extremely tall poles, side by side, which disappeared into the clouds.

"Of course, Wave likes this one only because it's a racing one," Beeze said. "You race to the top, remember the symbols, race down, and put in the symbols you memorized. It will either flash green if you're right or red if you're wrong! You do this ten times with different symbols. The one who gets the fastest time and most symbols right WINS!"

"Kind of like a *Survivor* challenge," she muttered under her breath, thinking of the TV show she liked. *Except for the flying part!*

"Beeze, come on!" Wave yelled over to her; he was already on the platform and at the bottom of one of the poles.

Beeze asked Skyler if she would like to go first, but she told Beeze to go ahead, and that she wanted to watch them. They raced up and down; sometimes (from their reactions) she could tell that they'd gotten the wrong symbol. It was easy to tell with Wave. He cried *"Noooooooooooo!"* Each and every time he put the wrong symbol in. It was an extremely close race—really too close to tell who had won. When they walked back over to where she was, they were both beaming and breathing heavy.

"Tie!" Wave wheezed out, high-fiving Beeze. They had both won a pin made out of silver wings.

"Give me a minute and I'll race you," Wave heaved, bending over, completely out of breath.

"No, no!" Skyler laughed, "I'm all good, take your time."

"I'll go with you if you would like to try it out," she heard a woman's voice say from behind her. Skyler spun around to see a beautiful fairy with pale blue eyes and long blue hair standing in front of her, wearing purple tights with dark purple swirls on them, and a casual purple tank top. Skyler gasped when she saw the fairy's huge turquoise hummingbird wings. The inside of her wings were patterns of swirls, in shades of turquoise! Still staring at her in awe, she thought, *I know you, but from where?* Before Skyler could answer her own question, she heard someone else's voice in her head say, *"My name is May."*

What the... Wait ... you can hear me? "Umm ... hi," Skyler said, embarrassed. She peered up to look at the beautiful fairy.

May giggled and said, "Hi Skyler." She looked behind her, "Hey Wave, hi Beeze!" May smiled over at them.

"Hey May!" Wave and Beeze answered in unison, still bent over and gasping for air.

"So do you feel like trying it?" May asked, as she nodded towards the game.

"Well ... we were supposed to digest our food," Skyler said, looking over at Wave with an I-told-you-so look. He looked green!

"Smart girl! How about the seahorse game? We can all play that one! And it's a sit-down game," May told them.

Everyone agreed with her, and slowly made their way back over to the games. Skyler couldn't help but stare at May's beautiful hummingbird wings. She dropped behind her to take a better look at them, but almost tripped over May's two longer tail-feathers, which trailed behind her when she walked. Skyler had to move to the side several times to avoid stepping on her feathers. She noticed that they had black symbols on both of them, but couldn't quite make the symbols out. May said hello to everyone she saw, and warmly hugged the other fairies.

The four fairies arrived at the water-squirting game. They aimed their seahorses towards tiny bull's-eyes. They pulled the triggers on the seahorses and as they squirted streams of water at their targets, they watched as each of their crabs raced up the painted undersea mural. Wave cheered his crab on throughout the whole race! They played the game until each of them had won a race each. Their prizes were small colourful, stuffed seahorses. After, May told them that she had to "fly, no pun intended!" She was part of the water show, and needed to get back to the pond to help out.

"May's so sweet. The water show is tonight at the pond; it's amazing!" Beeze exclaimed.

"She's awesome!" Wave said, watching May fly off. "Okay, now for the rides!" He had finally returned to his normal colour.

Skyler and Beeze followed Wave over to a roller coaster. They went on every roller coaster, all seven of them. Each one had different twists, turns, and loop to loops; one even went backwards! They went on the merry-go-round, bumper cars, the drop of doom, and a spaceship ride that swung in a circle that gradually climbed higher and higher. They did this until Wave's stomach started to growl with hunger again!

"I'm hungry; you guys want to head over to the tea tent?" he asked them.

"I could go for some tea!" Beeze answered.

"Sure," Skyler replied, even though she wasn't sure if she could stomach anything after all the rides they had been on.

She stopped walking when they approached a building that looked like a haunted house. She always loved going in them—even though she was often afraid of the unknown, and closed her eyes most of the time! *Well up until recently.* She had always made it through everyone single one, eyes closed or not.

Large letters above the entrance said: *FACE YOUR FEARS.*

"Wave and I still haven't tried that one," Beeze said with a voice that shivered.

"It's supposed to make your worst nightmares come to life … brrrr!" Wave said, wrapping his arms around himself and pretending to shiver.

"The main object is to see if you can conquer your fears," Beeze said.

"With no weapons!" Wave added. "It is all about inner strength; that's what the Queen told us," Beeze explained. "Once you can face your fears, you are more able to let them go."

"I think we should go into it together," Wave suggested.

"Oooooh, I don't know if I can," Beeze said, staring at the entrance.

"Is it all of our worst nightmares combined?" Skyler asked them.

"You can only see your own nightmares, and the same goes for us," Beeze answered.

"Yeah, but we'll be in there together at least," Wave said with sincerity.

The three of them stood there looking at the haunted house for several minutes.

Finally they looked at each other, and without a word, the three fairies walk over to the entrance of *FACE YOUR FEARS*.

"Okay, before we go in," Wave said, "we need a safety word, like caw-caw-caw-caw, and that will be the signal for us to abort! We can leave through the chicken door." She didn't care that Wave had called it a "chicken door." She was just happy that there was an early escape door at all! Beeze grabbed Skyler's hand; she was already scared, and inching slowly towards the door. "We don't have to go in Beeze," Skyler told her. Beeze was tightly squeezing her hand. Wave joined into the huddle, which made them all laugh.

"We've got each other," Wave whispered, as the three fairies entered the door.

He started to sing: "*Lean on me, when you're not strong,*" but Skyler swatted him on his arm. Little by little, still tightly squeezed, they made their way deeper into the house until they found themselves in a large room—a circle formed by glowing lights. A beam of light streamed down from the ceiling in the centre of the room. *It looks like a Star Trek beam,* Skyler thought to herself. "Beam me up, Scotty!" she heard Wave say from beside her, making them all laugh. They walked over into the centre of the light; an automatic rail rose up around them.

The walls lit up like an *IMAX* theatre, and the Queen appeared on every surrounding screen. "Welcome to Face Your Fears, you have come so far already in your quest," she said. The Queen floated in a forest, with her large swan wings extended. She continued, "What you are about to face cannot physically hurt or harm you in any way! It is for you alone to choose whether or not you face these fears. You have already faced a fear, just by entering here, and you should be very proud of yourselves. Believe in yourselves!" Her image flickered a little.

The Queen continued to give them instructions: Each of them had individual doors to their own journeys, and they had to go through them alone. "You are truly never alone," she said, right before the screen went completely black.

Three doors started to glow around their frames. Suddenly trails of dots lit up the ground to and from the doors, like a connect-the-dots puzzle! Three separate trails led towards the three fairies, and stopped in front of them. Looking down at the floor, Skyler saw a soft glowing dot in front of her feet. She followed the dots along the ground to her door, while Wave and Beeze went and stood in front of their own doors.

"Well it's been swell knowing you guys!" Wave said, only half-kidding. "Remember caw-caw-caw-caw is the safety word, and there's an exit door at the end of each room you go through. Now let's bring it into the middle," he said. He brought both of his hands into the middle, and waited there until Beeze and Skyler finally put their hands in too. "Goooooooooo team!" he yelled, pushing their hands up into the air.

"All right!" He jumped up and down like a boxer, moving his head from side to side. "We got this!"

Wave was humming the theme song from the movie *Rocky*, when he turned around and started fist pumping both arms in the air. Pounded his chest, he opened his door and walked through.

"Skyler?" Beeze said nervously.

"Yes Beeze?"

"I'm still a bit scared," Beeze said.

"Me too," Skyler said truthfully.

They turned to each other, hugging and wishing each other good luck. Then Skyler turned, stood in front of her door, and stared at it. *What's the worst thing that could happen?* she thought to herself, but really didn't want an answer. As she opened the door and walked into her chosen room, she found that it was mainly dark and quiet. Then she heard a musical jack in the box. *No, no, no, no!* She panicked. That sound only meant one thing to her: *clowns.* The tune grew louder and louder the deeper she went. The "chicken exit" was now to the right of her.

The tune kept *clinking* away, and she had a big decision to make. Skyler would bet anything that she was about to face her childhood fear of clowns. Now was the time, whether or not she had the courage to face it. As if her wings had read her mind, they gently wrapped around her shoulders. "Never alone..." she whispered, and took in a huge breath. She held that breath inside and quickly walked forward! The quicker she could face her fears, the quicker it would be over. What she saw instantly froze her with fear, losing her voice to call out *caw-caw-caw* to Wave or Beeze. She had already passed the *chicken exit*, and it slammed shut behind her!

There, in front of her, were over a hundred scary clowns! Some were popping out of jack-in-the-boxes, others rode tricycles or juggled, and some were even making animal balloons, and shooting each other out of cannons. Each clown performed different acts … all but one! She had just spotted her main fear when a little blonde girl ran by her. She was running away from something and hiding behind a crowd of clowns! The little girls eyes were filled with fear! Skyler followed the little girl's stare straight to *him!* This one clown was staring directly at Skyler, grinning eerily at her, with his long sharp fangs, black hollowed eyes, and smudged clown makeup.

Just then, the little girl took a chance to run and hide farther away from him. But the clown was too quick and saw the little girl making a break for it! He slunk towards the little girl, through the crowd of clowns.

No, no, no, this is not happening! Skyler thought, panicking and searching the room for the little girl. She spotted her at the far side of the room. The little girl was crouching down behind a cannon that was shooting clowns out, head first, into very large pies.

Skyler scanned the clowns, looking for *him.* And there he was! Moving like a predator, seeking his prey and staring directly at the canon. *OH NO! HE KNOWS WHERE SHE IS!* she screamed inside her head. Before Skyler even knew what she was doing, she bolted straight towards the little girl! She scooped her up into her arms and ran with her. Skyler's adrenaline kicked into high gear! She was a lot stronger than most, for her age. She tried flying, but a powerful force pushed her down and kept her grounded. So she weaved in and out of the crowd of clowns, until she no longer had the strength to carry the little girl. She hid them behind a rodeo barrel, with clowns still in them. Skyler poked her head out around the barrel to look for *him!* Instead, she heard a blood-curdling scream come from beside her. "The girl!" she cried out. Her heart was pounding. The little girl was gone! Skyler's blood boiled inside. She stood up tall and saw the little girl. Her eyes were tightly shut, and her tears were streaming down her face. The evil clown held the little girl in his clutches! She was struggling to break free.

"Let her go," Skyler said, barely in a whisper. The clown's grin grew even wider, exposing his long razor fangs, and he snickered at her. Skyler cleared her throat, straightened her posture, and held her ground. "I said, LET HER GO!!!!" she screamed at the top of her lungs. The clown's grin disappeared. He was staring at her with his dark eye-sockets. *He is not real; he is not real; he is not real …* she repeated this to herself. The clown was backing away, staring at her, and pulling the little girl with him into the crowd of clowns.

"STOP!" she yelled at him. A sly grin crossed his face, but this time it really made her mad. Bolting out from behind the barrel, Skyler ran towards them at full speed, stopping so close to them that she could actually smell the clown's foul breath.

"Eew! You need a breath-mint!" she told the evil clown. At this, his expression turned from evil to hurt. This took her by surprise! He let go of the little girl, and Skyler quickly grabbed her hand. "Thank you for setting me free," the little girl said, smiling up at her with innocent blue eyes.

The little girl was flickering like a light. Skyler looked around at all the objects and clowns; they were all starting to flicker. She saw the evil clown cup his hand, smell his own breath, and grimace. The rest of the images in the room, along with the little girl and the evil clown, suddenly vanished into thin air!

She waited for a few more minutes, just in case something reappeared. Looking around the room carefully, she confirmed that everything was gone. She had just faced one of her biggest fears, and she had won! At this realization, Skyler took a victory lap around the room. At the end of her victory lap, another door suddenly opened, and the room went pitch black. "Ah crap!" she muttered, but the floor lights quickly lit up. She followed them to another door, opened it, and stepped through.

Skyler was surprised to see Beeze slumped in a large lounge chair on the other side of the door! Beeze looked exhausted. The round room was softly lit, with six comfy lounge chairs, and Beeze was curled up in one. The chairs were arranged in a circle to face each other. Placed in the centre of the chairs was a wooden, oval-shaped table with an assortment of sandwiches, goodies, juices, and teas. Beeze opened her eyes and gave her a weak smile. "Hey, how did it go?" Beeze wearily asked her.

Skyler thought about it for a moment; the courage she had felt had even surprised her! She had been too worried for the little girl, and angry with the clown, to stay scared for long, and the other clowns hadn't even worried her. She had been too focused on helping the little girl to care about Stinky the clown or any of the other ones.

"Actually, better than I thought!" she said. "How about you?"

"Let's get some tea first, and then I'll tell you what happened," Beeze replied.

Apparently Beeze was terrified of bees! She had to face a room full of giant bees, flying around a room filled with giant sunflowers. Beeze had used the sunflowers to take cover from the bees. They swooped down at her, and she said that it felt like hours, hiding and running away from these bees. Beeze told her how she finally faced one of the bees. One had spoken to her and they became friends.

Just as Beeze was in mid-sentence about the rest of her nightmare, Wave came crashing through his own door. He saw the two of them, and came running towards them. Falling down onto his knees, Wave kissed the carpet. He looked up to the ceiling, breathing hard. He was soaking wet, with his head tilted back as though he couldn't hold it up any longer.

"So happy to be in this room!" he breathed out, still kneeling on the ground.

"That bad, huh?" Skyler asked.

"Dude, imagine deep dark waters, I mean D-A-R-K waters, surfing … put it together, and you get a fear of *What is in the water with you?* No fun at all," Wave said, shaking his head back and forth.

"Ah I get it, mine were clowns," Skyler told him.

"Clowns?" he asked, pausing for a moment. "Yep, I can see that; they are pretty scary." Wave was thumbing over towards Beeze. She was still curled up in her chair and her eyes were closed.

"Giant bees," Skyler whispered over to him.

"Only Beeze," he said, smiling over at her.

Beeze had fallen asleep in her lounge chair, so they let her rest. Skyler and Wave exchanged stories and high-fived one another. They also grew quite tired, and soon all three fairies were fast asleep.

"Morning sunshine!" Wave said to Skyler, tilting his teacup towards her.

"Morning? What?" Skyler yawned, but she felt refreshed.

"Actually, I think it's still afternoon-ish," Wave said, yawning, and he stretched out one arm from underneath a blanket.

Skyler noticed a soft baby blue blanket covering her body, and felt cozy. Wave got up and handed her a cup of tea. He started mixing some cold water with some of the boiled water in one large glass. Beeze was still sleeping. Wave crept over to her and put her hand into the glass, trying to play a practical joke on her.

"WAAAAAVE!" Beeze growled, startling Wave and making him fall backwards into his chair.

"Wow Beeze! You're like an angry bear when you wake up!" Wave exclaimed, and pretended to write on a notepad, "Note to self … Beeze not a morning person. Check."

"Blah, blah, blah," was all Beeze managed to say.

The three of them went over their fears again. During Wave's recap of how a shark bit off half his surfboard, a voice interrupted him, booming over the speakers in the room.

"Please remain seated for the rest of your ride. It is now time for you to sit back in your chairs. Thank you and enjoy the ride!"

They heard clicking noises, and at first Skyler thought that the walls were turning around them. In reality, it was the floor underneath them that turned. Wave's chair was the first to turn towards the open door and go through.

"Here we go again!" Wave yelled over the back of his chair, and waved at them.

Skyler's chair started to turn, moving slowly forward through the door, and into the darkness. At first, it reminded her of the Haunted House ride in *Disneyland*, when a ghost had appeared in between her and her mother when they were facing a mirror. *No mirrors so far!* She heard Beeze let out a small screech behind her. Wave's chair wasn't that far ahead of hers, and she could hear the ticking of his chair. They were gliding through a rain-forest, with the sound of rain, thunder, and lightning! *This is awesome*! Ahead, she spotted a bit of sunshine peeking through long drapes of fabric, with an exit sign above them. *Looks like a car wash!*

Wave went through the drapes, with his hands over his head, cheering. Skyler smiled at him, and did exactly the same as Wave! His chair was now turned to face hers, and he was saying, "Awesome!"

"I am not going back in there for a LONG time," she heard Beeze say from behind her. Skyler's chair parked right beside Wave's, and now she was able to see Beeze, who was shaking her head back and forth as she kept repeating, "A long time ... yes, a very long time before I ever go in there again!"

"The beginning of the ride was difficult for sure," Skyler told Beeze, "but we did it; we faced one of our fears, and look, we made it! Together and alone!"

Beeze smiled at this and exclaimed, "You're right! We should celebrate!"

"We can celebrate by watching the water show tonight: *The Journey*!" Wave cried.

"Skyler look!" Beeze cried, pointing to Skyler's bracelet. Skyler looked down to see a bright glow coming from her wrist.

"Beeze, Wave!" she cried out. Wave's wings were glowing, and so was Beeze's wrist.

Staring back down at her bracelet, Skyler noticed a new charm dangling, in solid silver: a little girl sleeping in a nightgown on top of a wolf's back. She looked up to see Wave opening his large wings and heard him gasped, "The waves are even bigger!!! Gnarly!"

"Two new beautiful bees," Beeze said, smiling and holding out her wrist to Skyler.

They decided to celebrate their courage by playing the very first game again: *Wings*. Skyler raced both of the fairies and won, both times!

Chapter 7

All of the living creatures in Piper's Pond were heading towards the pond for the water show. Skyler was busy taking it all in. Fairies flew, walked, drove go-karts, or surfed on small waves in the air! Fairies like B.W. flew by; gnomes walked past her, and so did talking animals. Two large blossom trees were giggling as they whooshed by her, and leaving behind trails of their pink petals. Everywhere she looked there was something new and colourful.

"Follow me dudettes!" Wave exclaimed, as he took to the sky. Skyler and Beeze followed him, flying up and towards a huge oak tree. They landed on a wooden platform big enough for a lot more fairies! Following Wave into a hollow part in the tree's limb, Skyler saw beanbag chairs along the floor of the oak, and thick quilts stacked on top of them. Beside each of the beanbags sat small baskets filled with fruits, chocolates, an assortment of popcorn, pretzels, nuts, and licorices, as well as drinks ... pretty much everything you needed for a show. And the overhang of the oak would protect them if it rained. It was pure luxury inside this old oak tree!

"This tree, by far, has the best view," Wave said dreamingly.

Skyler saw a dark shadow flying closer to them. She leaned up from her beanbag to see if she could get a better look. Looking over at Wave and Beeze, she could tell they had seen the shadow too, and didn't seem bothered by it. The shadow grew closer and she saw that it was a fairy dressed in a Ninja suit with gold trim— although she could only just make out what he was wearing. As he grew closer, she could see his wings. They were made out of branches, twigs, cobwebs, and fall leaves. The dark branches outlined his wings, and the tips were extended farther by twigs twisting and bending into Yin and Yang symbols at the ends. Leaves of orange hues, yellows, and bright reds lined the inside of his wings. Cobwebs covered the outside of them. As he glided onto the platform, his eyes were glowing a startling blue colour!

"Hey Mac! How's it hangin'?" Wave asked the Ninja.

"Hello Wave, may I join you guys?" he asked them politely.

"Oh yes Macbeth!" Beeze said, patting the beanbag beside her, and batting her dark lashes at him. "Come sit here."

"Thank you," he said, with a charming smile.

Cute! He sat down between Beeze and Skyler. Skyler was already stretched out on her beanbag with a blanket over her.

Other fairies found their own special spots. They were sitting in trees, or on cliffs, small clouds, or stars. Some even sat on blankets by the pond. You could see them twinkling when the sun went down. Several of the younger ones played games around the trees below.

Skyler heard a little girl's voice cry out, "Bobby is pulling on my blossoms again, Mom!" She looked down to see a little cherry blossom tree, whose branch arm was bent to her trunk. The little tree's face was smooth, but had a really annoyed look on it! She was staring up at an enormous cherry blossom tree! Her expression turned into a pout, and complaining, "Dad!"

A booming voice came out of the older tree, "Bobby, stop pulling your sister's petals!"

"Blossoms," the little cherry blossom tree corrected her father.

"Right, stop pulling your sister's blossoms, Bobby!" the father yelled over to his son, who was playing with his buddies. Skyler leaned farther over to see a small gnome, another blossom tree (not much bigger than the girl tree), a medium-sized weeping willow tree, a boy fairy with wings that looked like a superman cape, and a raccoon, all playing together.

"OKAY Dad!" he yelled over to them, "Come on sis, you're it!"

"Where's Mom when you need her?" the little girl tree huffed, and then went running back towards her brother and friends.

She was yelling, "Uh, um, Banjo, is it?" Then she suddenly stopped dead in her roots. The sound of thunder echoed all around them, and was followed by a loud boom! A display of fireworks lit up the sky!

"Woo hoo, it's starting!" Wave screamed, excitedly pointing towards the sky.

"Oooooh, I'm so excited!" Beeze said, squeezing Macbeth's arm.

The Ninja leaned over to Skyler, "By the way, a pleasure to meet you Skyler; my name is Macbeth, but you can call me Mac." His eyes twinkled through the slit of his ninja hood.

Skyler shook his hand and whispered back, "Likewise." They both turned to watch the firework display. There was something peaceful about Mac. She felt like she was hanging out with old friends. She leaned back into her beanbag, with a smile on her face, and enjoyed the fireworks.

They were the best fireworks she had ever seen in her life! They went on for over an hour, and each one was grander than the last. Some of the fireworks made 3D shapes: dragons, lions, unicorns, and soaring eagles, and they all seemed so real! Skyler and Beeze both pulled up their blankets when the 3D shapes flew almost straight at them. Wave cheered for his favourite ones!

There was a short intermission announced at the end of the fireworks, so the fairies took this time to eat snacks and have something to drink, chatting amongst themselves about the fireworks and which ones were their favourites.

"Each one was spectacular in their own way," Mac said, leaning back in his beanbag chair. He took off his hood, running his hand through his short, spiky blond hair, and popping a sucker into his mouth. Mac seemed to be aware of everything and everyone around him, watching with his startling blue eyes. Skyler guessed him to be a couple years older than her, and super cute. *No wonder Beeze is all flirty with him.* Beeze was sitting there staring at him.

"Mac is a walking fortune cookie! He's totally helped me out a few times, with his wisdom!" Wave said, nodding over to Mac, "I love you, man!"

Mac laughed out loud and replied, "Love you too, man!"

"Mac has a heart of gold," Beeze gushed, and squeezed his arm.

"Geeshh!" Wave exhaled. Skyler noticed a twinge of jealousy coming from Wave.

"So do you Wave!" Beeze said sincerely, trying to reassure him. "Don't you ever forget that." She gave Wave a flirtatious smile of his own, and this seemed to help the sudden mood swing.

"How is your journey so far?" Macbeth asked Skyler.

Skyler thought about it for a moment. She couldn't think of the proper words to explain her journey, and all she could say was, "Amazing!"

"Every journey has different roads; there is no right or wrong choice. Each is simply the one you needed to take at that time, to get where you are today." He paused for a moment and then continued, "Each road has many obstacles; it's how you react to them that matters. You have to figure out what is good for you or toxic for you."

"See what I mean about the fortune cookie!" Wave smiled over at Mac, and gave him a wink.

"That was beautifully said Mac," Beeze said with a sigh. Wave rolled his eyes at her.

Skyler nodded to him in agreement, and said (more to herself than to him), "Many journeys, many paths."

"Fortune cookies!" Wave managed to say, right before choking on a popcorn kernel that he'd thrown high in the air and caught in his mouth ... well, his throat.

The crowd went silent again, as the lights dimmed all around them.

Suddenly, blasting from the speakers, came the words, "*Just a small town girl ... living in a lonely world ...* " Skyler started giggling at the opening song, recognizing the opening lyrics of Journey's "Don't Stop Believing". She had lost track of how many times she and her mom had sung that song. She knew all the lyrics to it and started singing along. Everyone in Piper's Pond joined in. The four of them in the tree sang in full harmonization! Colourful sprays of water shot up and out of the pond to the rhythm of the music.

B.W. and her whale friends flew over to the centre of the pond, lining up side by side in the air. Dolphins with dragon wings glided over top of B.W and the rest of the whales. They were performing a magic show, sawing a whale in half, performing disappearing acts, water tricks, and acrobatic acts! All four fairies cheered really loud, calling out B.W.'s name as loudly as they could from the tree. At the end of their act, B.W. spun dramatically in the air and plunged into the water. After disappearing into the pond, a rainbow tornado spun over the top of the water. The next performers were the fairy mermaids she'd met earlier. They made beautiful streaks of colours and shapes in the air with their tails, much like the colours and images often seen through a kaleidoscope. They received lots of oooohs and aaaahs from the crowd.

"Look! May is up!" Beeze shouted.

May was hovering high above the pond. Her great humming-bird wings were expanded, and in her hands were two long, purple silk ribbons that descended from the starry sky and almost touched the top of the pond. "Wow!" Skyler gasped. May was gracefully flipping and turning with the ribbons. She had seen Pink, one of her favourite singers, perform an Aerial Silk act once, and she'd found it breathtakingly beautiful. May's act was even more wondrous.

"She's amazing!" Wave said in awe, staring at May with wide eyes.

"Ahem!" Beeze said, pretending to clear her throat.

"So are you Beeze," Wave said to Beeze, without tearing his eyes away from May.

May descended farther down the ribbons. She displayed many extravagant tricks in the centre of the stage. She hovered with her wings fully extended, and the moonlight as her background. Her toes were just skimming the pond. Images of wolves formed on the surface of the water, and howls cried out. May gracefully folded in her wings, and sat on an orange quarter moon that hung down, gradually being pulled farther up, and away from the crowd below. Looking out towards the stars, her wings trailed beneath the moon. The crowd exploded with applause.

"Holy crap, Batman! Now I know where I recognize her! My mom's fairy tattoo!" Skyler cried out.

"What?" Wave asked. He was still standing up and clapping.

"My mom's tattoo!" Skyler yelled to him, over the applause.

"Cool, your mom has a tattoo! Awesome!" Wave yelled back over to her.

"It could be," Macbeth said. She was surprised by Mac's answer and asked him, "How? How could it be?"

"Things happen for a reason," he answered.

"Not helpful. May *is* a tattoo on my mom's back. The tattoo *is* May."

"Maybe they are part of a similar creation," Mac said.

"Mac, sometimes I just need a straight answer," she continued. "I know, I know … sometimes there *are* no straight answers, and things just happen!" He was feeling more and more like an older brother to her.

His eyes filled with wisdom, kindness, and love. "Exactly," he said with a nod.

"Fortune Cookie," Wave quietly sang out under his breath, staring straight ahead towards the pond.

The grand "Journey" show came to an awesome ending, with another round of incredible fireworks, but this time the King was conducting them in the air. *He definitely looks a lot like Zeus, but with cool black crow wings. Awesome!*

"Hello!" Sally sang out to them. She was carrying a tea tray filled with goodies in her arms. The Queen gracefully flew beside Sally, carrying a tray of her own with tea on it. Wave and Macbeth stood up right away to help them. The Queen and Sally handed the trays over to the boys before they both glided down onto the oak floor.

"YUM!" Wave said, smacking his lips at the sight of the tea sandwiches, scones, and small pastries.

"Hello Macbeth, did you enjoy the fireworks and shows?" the Queen asked him, and gave him a hug.

"It was amazing, my Queen," Mac said, hugging her back. Then he stepped back and bent at his waist, taking the Queen's hand and kissing it.

"You know Macbeth, you don't need to do that," the Queen said to him, giving him a gentle smile.

"I know," Macbeth said in return; he blushed, and kissed the Queen's hand again anyways.

"Well thank you Macbeth, so kind of you," the Queen said, and gently straightened Mac up into a standing position.

Mac continued to blush; this made Beeze turn red with jealousy.

"Did you have a good night too, Beeze?" the Queen asked her, as she wrapped her arms around her. Beeze's colour returned to normal and she squeezed the Queen back.

"It was a beautiful night," Beeze said quietly, still hugging the Queen with her eyes closed. Skyler, was sipping on the tea that Sally had given to her. She was thinking that the Queen and Beeze looked more like mother and daughter. Watching them made her think of her own mom. She was really starting to miss her, and wished that she could be sharing this experience with her.

All of a sudden, a swirl of wind started spinning quickly around her, like being in the centre of a tornado! Skyler was starting to feel unbalanced and whoozy! She accidentally dropped her teacup. *Oh No!* She had a horrible feeling, as though she were going to pass out, and her eyes went out of focus. Everything and everyone around her blurred then, followed by a blinding white light!

Chapter 8

Skyler batted her eyes against a stream of sunshine peering through turquoise curtains with white daisies on them ... she was in her room, snuggled warmly in her bed, and smiling because she didn't have to get up to go to school. Her heart almost jumped out of her chest when the memories came flooding in: Piper's Pond! She sat straight up, looking behind her for her wings. A sudden sadness settled in her heart; her wings were gone. Touching each shoulder, she gently stroked where her wings had once been. She let out a huge sigh! *They were so magnificent and so strong!*

Looking over at her night table, she saw a small figurine: a howling wolf made of silver, with wings that were similar to her own. She could feel a slight tugging, and a warm tingling from her shoulders. Skyler reached down and stroked the small wolf's wings; they felt like hers had.

Skyler could hear music coming from the kitchen, and voices! *Mom is talking to someone in the kitchen!* She bolted out of bed and out of her bedroom, slowing up just before entering the kitchen. Listening to the voices in the kitchen, she tried to identify them. She knew she would know Jazz's voice for sure! She still felt strange without wings, but wore the same clothes as the day before. Skyler gasped, realizing that she was still wearing the silver charm bracelet on her wrist! Raising her bracelet up to eye level, she caught a glimmer of white light flying through the air beyond it! The light stopped right in front of her. It was May! Through the small white light, she saw May waving at her! Then May quickly flew off towards her mom.

MOM! Skyler lit up with happiness at the sight of her mom! Her mom's back was turned towards her, she was dancing to some music, and busily organizing something on the counter-top. She was wearing pale blue lounge pants and a grey long sleeve shirt with an open back. May flew towards her mother's back, then turned and blew her a 3D kiss that landed right on her nose. Then she vanished into her mom's back! The fairy tattoo on her mother's back twinkled, with a fairy sitting peacefully on an orange quarter moon. *What the ...?!!*

"Uh ... Mom?" Skyler called, trying to get her mother's attention above the music.

Her mom spun around, a huge smile spreading across her face before she came running over to Skyler, and grabbed her into a tight embrace. They were in a bear hug for a long time. "So Mom, you have some explaining to do."

"Tell me all about your trip!" her mom said, while grabbing the breakfast from the counter, placing chocolate chip pancakes, an assortment of fruits, and juice on the table.

"We can chat over breakfast or all day or however long you want, but if you are too tired I understand." Her mom smiled over at her.

Too tired? I just woke up!

She had so much to tell her mom and so much to ask her, but Skyler was happy to see her mom. Looking out the window at the fairy garden, they both greeted it in unison: "*Good morning!*" This time the garden flashed with lights, extremely close to the window. Her mom reached over, cracking open the side window a little, and Skyler heard tiny voices yelling good morning and speaking over each other.

"Way to be subtle you guys!" said her mom in a loud voice. Excited fairies gathered around the window, and her mom gave them sarcastic thumbs up!

"Dudette!" Wave yelled; he was surfing in the air, near the window closest to her. Giving her two thumbs up, he yelled, "Catch ya later!" Then he surfed off. Beeze appeared in the window next. She leaned over and kissed the glass, leaving a tiny red lipstick mark. Skyler placed her index finger on the tiny mark. Beeze placed both of her tiny hands on the other side of the glass.

"Mom? Can I go out to see them?" she asked. Beeze waved at her, before flying off in the same direction as Wave.

"Of course, anytime! But first, let's eat and you can tell me exactly what happened at the Pond." Her mom continued,

"Besides, those guys weren't supposed to show themselves all at once. They were just too excited to see you again!"

Her mom continued to watch the fairies stop at the window; they were waving, showing off, and making funny faces.

"Mom? How …?" She was waving her hand towards the whole garden scene.

"I'm being honest when I say that I am really *not* too sure exactly. Well I have nothing to say that will really make any sense and I really don't want to overload you with too much. I started working on the garden as a distraction, a focus, and an escape. The pond is somewhere I can pour all my emotions into … unconditionally, good and bad. The more I expanded the garden, the more odd and unexplainable things started to happen. A year after your father passed away, Jazz appeared with another fairy to look after you for the day. Your Aunt Christine came that same day too! I mean it when I say that it took them a *very* long time to convince me that you were in extremely good hands. That day was my very first trip to Piper's Pond. Unexplainable and extraordinary things *can* happen! And I realized I was more than okay with it. I found a different type of happiness. I found *me* again. And for some reason, they named the pond after me. One day, I will explain that a bit more."

Skyler was staring into the fairy garden, watching a tiny cherry blossom tree skipping along and leaving trails of tiny, pretty pink blossoms. "According to the King and Queen, stranger things happen." Her mom laughed at the thought of this.

Fairies kept appearing in the window. Skyler was thinking about Uncle Tomas and the Queen when she heard her mom's voice calling her. She looked back over at her mom. The King and Queen were hovering between her and her mom, bright gold beams shining all around them and making them look like one bright star! Uncle Tomas was behind the Queen with his hands placed on her shoulders. His large black wings swayed, and the Queen's swan wings were pushing back against her husband. They were both brightly smiling at her. *How beautiful they both look!*

Skyler caught a glimpse of a bird's nest on the King's head, making her burst out laughing!

"Another play, Uncle Tom?" she giggled at him.

"Oh, they are going all out on this one!" he laughed, bending over slightly so that she could see the mom crow sitting happily on her eggs! He continued, "I have to be extra careful with this crown!"

The Queen flew over to Skyler, and planted a small kiss on her forehead. "You look beautiful!" the Queen told her. The King also gave her a gentle kiss on her forehead, but then he flew over to tweak her nose. "Got your nose!" he teased her, and then placed the pretend nose back. Looking like a proud father, he gently patted the side of her nose, and then flew back over to his Queen's side.

"Thank you both so much," Skyler said to them, barely in a whisper, and with happy tears in her eyes.

"Oh sweetheart, we are always here for you; please, come visit us real soon!" the Queen told her with an eager smile.

"But only if you keep your grades up!" Uncle Tom added, and winked at her mom. The King and Queen kissed her mom's forehead too. Uncle Tomas bowed and the Queen curtsied to her mom. "You guys!" her mom complained, giving them both a playful nudge with her fingertip, followed with her own exaggerated bow to them. Uncle Tomas turned back before following his Queen out the window. He told Skyler, "See you soon! Visit us anytime!" The rest of the fairies who had gathered by the window flew off after the King and Queen, and disappeared back into the garden.

"Mom, can we just chill out on the couch and watch movies?" Skyler suddenly felt exhausted, and said, "I don't know why I feel so tired. I just woke up!"

"Sure, I'm up for a movie," her mom said. "This I do know! Fairy form to human form, and vice versa, takes a lot out of you for the first few times. But you will adjust, in time."

"So I can become a fairy … any time I want?" Skyler asked.

"Well, there are some rules to follow, but other than that … you betcha!" her mom answered. "So what type of movie are you in the mood for?"

They headed into the living room, grabbing their blankets and snuggling up on the couch. Skyler leaned her wrist on her mom's shoulder, so she could take a closer look at her charm bracelet. A *Walking Dead* marathon was on the TV, so she left it on. Her mom was carefully looking at each of her charms.

Partway through watching the episode, they both fell asleep on the couch.

Chapter 9

Skyler woke up to the *Walking Dead* still playing on the TV. Her mom was sound asleep and Skyler was lying against her stomach. Quietly, without disturbing her mom, she pushed herself up, and got up from the couch. After pulling the blanket up over her mother's shoulders, she headed to the kitchen. The numbers and arms on the moon clock in the kitchen were glowing: 3:50 am. *Wow! I slept pretty much all day!* Sitting down on the bench beneath the clock, she grabbed one of the fairy pillows, and hugged it tightly to her body. Wrapping her arms around her knees, and the pillow, Skyler looked out the window at the pond. The solar lights along the fairy gardens and pathway twinkled. It was so quiet in the kitchen, and out in the garden.

Such pretty solar lights ... wait solar lights? Solarlite? The thought came to her suddenly. *Wait ... I never met anyone called Solarlite! Did I? The ticket was signed Solarlite!* She searched her memories, and tried to remember if she had met anyone by that name at Piper's Pond. Her bracelet was starting to glow in two different spots and two different colours, a sea blue and bright yellow! Then the glows disappeared. It took a moment for her eyes to adjust in the darkness, and she could only barely make out the two new charms that suddenly appeared. Skyler ran to the bathroom and flicked on the light. She was beaming at the sight of her two new charms: a small bee and a surfboard! *Beeze and Wave! They are going to be so happy when they see these!*

Later she would ask her mom about Solarlite. Walking quietly back into the living room, she settled back down onto the couch, and curled back up with her mom. She gradually fell back to sleep again with the TV still on, and a smile on her face.

"Check it out Beeze!" Wave whispered over to Beeze. She was trying to tug the blanket up over Skyler's shoulders. Beeze flew over to where Wave stared at Skyler's charm bracelet. He swiftly covered Beeze's mouth, before she could let out a joyful scream. She saw the bee charm on Skyler's bracelet, and was eagerly pointing at it.

"B-b-b … bee," Beeze muttered through Wave's fingers.

"Shhhhh! Let them sleep; Skyler needs it before we go on more adventures." Wave smiled sheepishly at Beeze and winked at her. "Maybe we could go back to *Face Your Fears,*" Wave said, in his spooky voice.

Skyler woke up at the sound of their voices, but kept her eyes tightly closed. She didn't want to scare them away, plus they were so cute together.

Beeze shot Wave a stern look, and once he had removed his hand from her mouth, whispered loudly to him, "Very funny! Ha ha!"

They finished pulling up the blanket together.

"Look Beeze, I'm a giant bee!" Wave teased, hovering in front of the TV screen. He screamed when he turned and saw a zombie on the screen!

Beeze giggled and said, "Race ya back!" They went zooming off into the kitchen, and Skyler heard a *thunk* sound against a window.

"Not again, Wave! You okay?" Beeze asked him, with concern.

"Who put that there?" Wave asking loudly, "Okay, from here ... go!"

Skyler waited a moment, before letting out a giggle.

"He does that every time and he never gets hurt, but he does it every time," her mom said with her eyes closed. "And by every time, I do mean e-v-e-r-y time!" Skyler propped herself up on her elbow, looking at her mom. She was rolling her eyes, and they broke out into hysterical laughter on the couch. "See! I told ya! I knew they were awake!" Wave whispered to Beeze. They had raced back into the living room, and were hiding behind the snow globe on the wooden hearth above the corner fireplace. Inside the globe was a picture of Skyler and her mom. In the picture, her mom was smiling down at her precious baby in her arms.

"So did I! But look Wave," Beeze said, gesturing over to Skyler and her mom, "just look at them. They are so darn cute."

Thunk!

"Ouch!" Wave yelped, having hit his head on the globe after trying to get a better view of them.

"Really? Again?" Beeze asked him, with wide, disbelieving eyes.

"Hello Beeze and Wave, you can come out. We're awake," Piper gently told them, through her giggles.

"Woo hoo! To more adventures and b-e-y-o-n-d!" Wave flew out from behind the snow-globe, with a flying style that was a combination of Superman and Buzz Lightyear! He stopped in mid-air and stared at Skyler's mom! "Oh, oh, here we go again!" he cried.

"Mom! Look!" Skyler yelled. She saw a cluster of bright lights, floating extremely close to her mom!

"Very funny Uncle Tomas … very funny!" Piper yelled, with a scolding finger pointing towards the sky. She quickly jumped up from the couch, and moved away from the lights.

"Stand back, ladies and gentleman, you are about to see quite the show!" Wave said, flying farther away from Piper.

A huge flash of light blinded them all, just for a moment. Skyler was staring directly at her mom with her mouth hanging open. Her mom looked … *AWESOME!* She was still human size, but with two pure white wolf wings stretching from one side of the living room to the other!

"Ta-da!" Piper exclaimed, trailing her fingers gently along her wings, and smiling at them.

All of them at once started to laugh so hard that it filled the entire house, joined by faint echoes of a howling wolf, the roar of a lion, and the growl of a bear!

"Let's sing a song!" Wave cried out.

Oh no, not again!

"MOMMMM!"

About Me

A little about me with quizzes asked throughout the years by my daughter:

Where can you be found on a Saturday night?
Chillin' watching movies and under blankets (especially if they are spooky).

What type of music do you listen to?
Every type...well, almost.

What movie will you never stop loving?
Army of Darkness.

What is the animal that best represents you?
A Wolf.

If you could describe yourself in one word, what would it be?
Dreamer.

Are you afraid of the dark?
I am afraid of what is in the dark.

What is your ideal way to spend the summer?
Camping.

Typically, how much make-up do you wear?
Just some mascara and lip stuff.

Favorite sports?
Kickboxing, mountain biking, swimming...really any sports.

What is your greatest accomplishment?
My children.

Favorite place to write?
Anywhere in nature!

What is the quote you put in your Grade 12 yearbook?
"Life is either a daring adventure or nothing," by Helen Keller.

Look for the Sequel:

Piper's Pond
The Unwritten Fairytale